ADVANCED PRAISE

"Sadika inspires me to be a better human being. Her ability to show me humanity's challenges and skillfully help me to experience through her eyes, stories and speeches how everyday people choose to overcome those challenges give me hope."

– Tim Gard, National Speaker Association Hall of Fame

"Sadika Kebbi's richly detailed and brutally honest writing challenges and disturbs readers by putting us face-to-face with human beings at their worst. In some stories, she takes us deep into the impoverished Tripoli neighborhood Bab Al-Tabbaneh, a place she knows well through her own volunteer work, to examine the lives of characters long infected with debauchery and lewdness. We meet men and women who have lost any sense of moral regard for others and their innocent victims in her achingly beautiful portrayals. She opens our eyes to the bleakest of lives and forces us to look at them with compassion."

– Sandra Whitehead is a journalist, author, and academic. She teaches at Marquette University in Milwaukee, Wisconsin, USA. where she created the Center for Peacemaking

"As a teacher, Sadika instilled sound knowledge and critical thinking in her students. On the several occasions, when she brought her students to GNK Foundation facilities and events, her students' admiration and appreciation for her were so apparent. They looked at her as their role model and she treated them with respect, firmness and love. Thanks to her, many of her students are now volunteers in GNK foundation."

–Dr.Adlette Inati, Professor, School of Medicine, Lebanese American University; Pediatric Hematologist/Oncologist at Boston Children's Hospital and Post-Doctoral Fellow at John Hopkins University

"Sadika was one of those few unorthodox teachers. She always thought out of the box, and she always delivered her message in a creative way, and mostly through hands-on activities which enabled

for The Hidden Face of Scheherazade

us to learn and apply our knowledge not only in class or in projects but also in our daily life. Sadika wasn't only a classroom teacher, but also a life coach. We shared our pain and joy with her. She was always there when we needed her, and she provided advice and solutions. She was one of the sweetest things that came my way as a high school student and as a child in general. My dad passed away back in June 2006 during the revision week and she was so sweet to bring my friends over from Tripoli to Batroun and take us out for dinner. She helped me out in one of my hardest times, and I feel she deserves a special thank you."

– Dr.Wissam El Helou, Ph.D. in information technology

"I owe my life to my mother, other than that being literally true, my mother had a huge impact on the person I am today. She was the kind of person who would engross herself in community service, whether it was with the poor, the sick, the dying, or any kind of person who needed help. However, the community service was not the only thing she had to take care of. She was going through her M.A. studies too, while taking care of her family. The hard work she does, going through life, inspired me to be a better human being, and I am deeply convinced that I have what it takes to contribute to the university as much as it will contribute to my education, my personality, and most importantly my future success."

– Rami Kamareddine, Chemical Engineer and Theta Healer

"You have engraved hope, faith and success in my mind. You have shown me light; you changed my life forever. You taught me a verb so strong, the verb was 'be'. I want you to know you set me free. You were never ahead to lead my path, but you were always beside me to soothe my wrath."

– Wafic Ryan Mikati, Sound Designer and Composer

Also by Sadika Kebbi

- Wrote an article on " Little Reed," published in *Home, The Soul of Lebanon, Magazine* in 2019.

- Wrote an article on "Appreciating the Art of Caricature Drawing with Hamed Kabbara," published in *Home, The Soul of Lebanon, Magazine* in 2018

- Wrote an article on "A Generation of People with Disabilities", published on Now Lebanon, online news website, on 2015-11-16.

- Wrote an article on "Souk al Tayeb," for *The Arab Weekly*, published by Al Arab Publishing House, on 2015-6-26.

- Wrote a review on Salma Hayek's "The Prophet," for *The Arab Weekly* published by Al Arab Publishing House, on 2015-5-15.

- Research Paper, "The Impact of Sectarianism and Intolerance on the Workplace in Lebanon," published by the *Academic American Scholarly Research Journal*, April 2013, Volume 5, Special Issue.

- "And the Stories Unfold" at the First Festival of Stories at AUB (American University of Beirut), article on the Festival of Storytelling held at AUB on 12-12-2012, published in *The Daily Star*, and on AUB's website.

- Research Paper, "The Impact of Prophet Muhammad's Misconceived Sunnah on the Traditional Muslim's Lifestyle in Tripoli, Lebanon," published by the *Academic American Scholarly Research Journal*, September 2012, Volume 4, Number 5, Issue.

- Academic book, "The Temptations of the Flesh in Madame Bovary and the Awakening,", published by LAP/ Lambert Academic Publishing, 2011.

The Hidden Face of
SCHEHERAZADE

*stories from
behind the veil*

Sadika Kebbi

"The truth was a mirror in the hands of God. It fell, and broke into pieces. Everybody took a piece of it, and they looked at it and thought they had the truth."
—Mawlana Jalal-al-Din Rumi

To my children Rana, Abed El Kader, Ramzi and Rami, may you always put the pieces of the mirror together to see the truth and unveil it to make this world a better place.

CONTENTS

FOREWORD

By Lorraine Taylor

Speaker, Author (Be Brand YOU),
Coach, and Communication Specialist

My introduction to Sadika Kebbi was witnessing her gift as a storyteller on the big stage in Dubai that showcased the talents of the top ten speakers in the Arab world. I was captured by her eloquence and the way she wove a mesmerizing, meaningful message into a personable, relatable story. Sadika's skill and talent as a storyteller help her transmit messages that penetrate our hearts and interlace our souls. She links all her story participants together with the commonality of their humanity.

Not long ago, I had the memorable opportunity to travel to Lebanon to learn its history, both the history of the ancient past and the history being made in the present. I learned that history by walking through the streets, by hearing the voices of the people, and through these stories that Sadika told of the lives that walked alongside us on the same pathways.

As you read each story, you will be whisked away to the streets of Tripoli and transported into the life of each character. It is there that barriers to true understanding will crumble, connecting you to the souls of these people that beg to be heard.

There is no doubt that, for Sadika, the writing of this book was a labour of love.

For you, the reader, it will change something at the deepest level of your being and connect you to the human inside of you.

"We are all different. There is no such thing as a standard or run-of-the-mill human being, but we share the same human spirit."

— Stephen Hawking

A Glossary of Arabic Words and Names

- **Abu** In Lebanon, it is customary to call men by the name of their eldest male child. "Abu" means "the father of."
- **Afandee** Sir
- **Al Kabr** An underdeveloped area in North Lebanon, located amidst a graveyard. In fact, the Arabic word "Kabr" means "grave."
- **Amina** A woman's name, meaning "safe"
- **Amo** Uncle
- **Aⁿdalusian** Refers to the Moorish culture
- **Argileh** A hubble-bubble; a form of the hookah in which the smoke passes through water, creating a bubbling sound.
- **Beb El Tebbeneh** An underprivileged area in Tripoli
- **El-hamdulillah** Thanks be to God
- **Habeebtee** My love (referring to a female)
- **Hala ya hala** Welcome, welcome
- **Kafan** The white cloth in which Muslims wrap their dead
- Koufias The black and white squared head coverings used by men to protect them from the sun
- **Labneh** A dairy product similar to yoghurt but more condensed
- **Lira** The Arabic for pound
- **Mou'ezen** The sheikh who leads and intones the call to prayer in a mosque
- **Nabrije** Another term for the hookah pipe
- **Sahteyn** Wishing someone to enjoy his/her food or drink
- **Tripoli** A city located in North Lebanon
- **Umm (or Um)** In Lebanon, it is customary to call women by the name of their eldest male child. "Umm" means "the mother of."
- **Umm Kalthum** A famous Egyptian singer
- **Zareef** An area in Beirut where a large public school was established by the government, and which was used, in 1978, to shelter refugees from Southern Lebanon.

1

Between Dreams and Reality

Fatima threw her heavy bulk onto the chair next to the kitchen table. Her breathing came labored and heavy as she smoked what must have been her tenth cigarette. Waving her hand before her, she drew swirling shapes with the floating, opaque smoke. "A villa by the seashore," she thought to herself, "or, maybe, a chalet deep within the cedar forest. Better yet, a fabulous apartment in downtown Beirut!"

Fatima looked at her reflection in the stainless-steel pot left on the one-eyed stove. A middle-aged reflection stared back at her with insolence. She tilted her head, leaned forward and stuck her nose to its cold surface. She licked the pot from bottom to top and then leaned back again into her chair. While her fingers traced her smeared image, she muttered to herself. If anyone else had been there, they would have found the words incomprehensible.

Fatima's dreams dissipated once she extinguished her fifteenth cigarette. She dragged her heavy mass through the kitchen and headed toward the long, narrow corridor. Only her body was aware that she was tightly holding onto an empty bottle of Johnny Walker Black. The corridor was dimly lit. The doors of the two bedrooms were locked but from their keyholes escaped a red light that stealthily crept along the walls of the hallway and then spread onto its ceiling. Fatima pressed her ear to the door of the first room where muffled voices could be heard. Her heart danced to the squeaking of a bed and a man's heavy breathing. Then, a knowing silence filled her ear with its deafening music.

Feeling content to her core, she tiptoed toward the door of the second room and again cemented her ear to its chilly wood. For a few minutes, Fatima could not discern a sound. Then, the rustle of crispy sheets resounded in the house followed by a terrible shriek that ripped the deadly quietness of the place, echoing the everlasting sin of Eve. A satisfied smile distorted Fatima's face. She treaded back softly to the kitchen, nodding her head and shaking her massive form to a loud rhythmic tune which only she could hear.

"Money, money, money, is a widow's dream,
Daughters, daughters, daughters are a mother's means,
One sixteen and the other eighteen
Their ripe bosoms shake coins out of men's pockets
One drink and one swing and money in my lap clink
Money, money, money is a widow's dream."

Fatima resumed her prior position on the chair. She held yet another cigarette between two nicotine-stained fingers while her dreamy gaze ventured down the dark hallway. When the two men stepped out of the rooms, the fat woman searched their faces, wrinkle by wrinkle, seeking a sign that could dissipate the clouds of her foggy sky. Then, the sudden miracle of green banknotes tore through her murky firmament and landed softly on her kitchen table. Fatima reached out and grabbed the dollars while both her teenage daughters rushed to the bathroom to clean up their mother's mess.

2

Business Deal

After a long and nerve-racking day at work, mostly the result of troubles caused by Fadi, his demanding boss, Mahmud walked into his quiet house. He was a tall, sturdy man but his black, frizzy hair grew in all directions and his bushy eyebrows gave him an unfriendly look. As for his honey-brown eyes, they were extinct; they seemed lifeless and glazed. His hooked nose, his thin lips, and his crooked teeth added to his grotesque appearance.

The young man headed straight to the tiny, narrow bathroom he shared with his wife and daughter. He washed his sweaty hands and splashed his face with cool tap water before sneaking into the bedroom where his family slept. He tiptoed up to the dark-brown closet. With great care, he opened one of its drawers, chose a navy-blue pajama and started to undress.

In no hurry, Mahmud unbuttoned his shirt and tossed it onto the beige and stained divan that sat against the wall facing the king-size bed. He stopped unzipping his pants to scratch the scar that had dug a trench into his left shoulder. His fingers traced the rough, blemished skin as his father's detestable memory fondled and tormented his thoughts. The life-altering event had disfigured his face, consumed his heart and drained his soul.

Mahmud chewed his lips and cracked his knuckles; the ten-year old boy was back again. He remembered that he was rummaging the fridge for something to satisfy his hunger when the intoxicated Abu Mahmud roared in, ranting and raving and smashing. By the time Abu Mahmud turned to leave, his helpless child was drowning in a pool of his own blood. Mahmud held his head between his hands in an attempt to stop the flow of remembrance before collapsing, exhausted and shattered, on the settee.

A soft sound attracted his attention. His plump wife rolled over to her right side followed by his daughter who snuggled tightly against her mother. A sudden grin brightened Mahmud's features. In a moment, he realized that his daughter was the answer to all of his problems. He rose from his seat, approached the bed and stood, looking down at Khadija, his five-year-old. She was perfect, every man's dream. Her green, wide eyes were entrancing. Her soft translucent skin invited touch. Khadija was his ticket to wealth. She was exactly what Fadi, his boss, longed for. Mahmud fell asleep and, for the first time since he could remember, dreamt.

With the first rays of the morning sun, Khadija, light on her feet, ran straightaway to her playroom where her dollies awaited her. Her loose, pink nightgown bounced along with her in undulating movements. Her long, thick, black hair joined in the bouncing.

As she did every morning, Khadija first peeked through the keyhole to assess the situation. She gazed at her playfellows for a few seconds while preparing her daily scenario in her little head. She, then, opened the door and screamed, "I got you! I saw you! You're being naughty! Fifi, you were biting Omar's hand! Omar, you were pinching her. That is unacceptable! As for you, Miss Loulou, you were laughing your head off at their misery. You should've interfered and stopped them from fighting. And, you, my dearest Teddy, I saw them kicking your butt. Come to mama, come to me, my sweet baby, oh, I love you so much. Don't worry, they will be grounded for the day and you will keep me company. As for the rest of you—Fifi, Omar, and Miss Loulou—you will not leave this room. You will not have any treats today. You will not watch T.V. or even attend tea parties. Do you hear me?"

Khadija cuddled Teddy while she gazed with malice at the rest of her dolls. She turned her head to greet her mother who was standing by the door, observing her daughter's theatrical performance. Samira winked at her and then proceeded to the kitchen to prepare breakfast. She kept an ear out for Khadija and, as she did so, could hear her daughter alternate between chatting with her toys and reprimanding them.

Mahmud woke up to the morning hubbub which, today, especially, made him happy. He felt an excitement that nearly gave him an erection. He was proud that he had, finally, found a way to settle the present, troubling business deal, as well as many other deals to come, with his superior.

Mahmud leaned his head against the bed's dark wood and drifted off to that day in the park. He was having coffee with his boss, Fadi.

"Hey, Mahmud, check out this sweet, little piece of pie! Brrrrrr!"

"You mean the blond toddler over there? She's only a baby."

"Believe me; they're best at this age. They smell like heaven; they sound like angels and they taste like honey."

Fadi choked on his words. His body rocked from head to toe; his face turned red. The poker face he wore like a mask, betraying neither joy nor sadness, melted away.

"Wait until he checks out my little piece of pie!" Mahmud thought to himself as he went to check on his daughter. He found her talking silliness to those dolls she called Fifi, Omar, Miss Loulou and Teddy.

Khadija sensed her father's glassy stare piercing through her. She crouched and tried her best to hide among her toys in order to avoid interacting with him. He always gave her the creeps.

She had never liked her father and preferred to stay away whenever he was around. You might say she even loathed him. She didn't know why, exactly, but her antipathy was, mainly, due to this blank look of his. She always tried to discover the person who hid behind those inert irises but, to this point, had always failed. She never saw him smile, laugh or even cry. She wondered what touching her father might feel like but she never even dared to come near him, and he, in turn, never offered a hug, a kiss or a touch. Today, he seemed especially opaque and that made him seem even more terrifying. To escape the cruel, freezing eyes that roved over her tiny figure, Khadija clasped Teddy hard against her chest, buried her face in Fifi's tiny lap and covered the back of her neck with Omar.

Mahmud grinned to himself at the child's maneuvers. Self-confident and satisfied, he shaved, showered, dressed, gobbled up his breakfast and left the house without bidding his wife and daughter goodbye, as usual.

Samira and Khadija were used to Mahmud's negligence. At first, his behavior gave Samira a fit but, by now, she didn't even care anymore. She was raised to be a woman. She was brought up to sacrifice herself so that her marriage could survive, so that her child would not grow up without a father. In her head, Samira could always hear the words of her great-grandmother, grandmother and mother, "The female should be the submissive spouse in the relationship or else the family will perish. A woman's place is by her husband's side, no matter what." Mother and daughter nibbled at the remainder of breakfast, each engrossed in her own thoughts. Samira pondered the advice of her female ancestors while Khadija was deciding to give Fifi, Miss Loulou and Omar another chance.

Meanwhile, Mahmud was on his way to his office, on

his way to Fadi to close that business deal. He parked his car, hurried to his superior's office, knocked at its door, and stepped in. Fadi was seated behind his desk, his bulging stomach almost resting on its top. Upon Mahmud's entrance, Fadi raised his head from what he was reading, signaled the man to take a seat and resumed his evaluation. Mahmud knew perfectly well that he had to wait until Fadi let him know he could address him. He observed the bulky man seated in front of him and all he could see were successful business deals. Fadi lifted his red eyes and stared back at Mahmud as if questioning his surveillance.

"I was thinking of inviting you over for dinner at my place to introduce you to my wife and daughter," said Mahmud. Upon hearing the word "daughter," Fadi dropped the papers he was holding and answered,

"Sure, sure, I'll be more than honored to meet your family."

"Okay, then. I'll call Samira and tell her to prepare a nourishing meal for us men. See you this evening then."

"Huh, by the way, how old is your daughter?"

Mahmud smiled, confident that Fadi had taken the bait, "Khadija is five years old, and she is a very smart and wonderful girl, you will enjoy her company."

"Great! I'll get her a nice gift, one suitable for her age."

"You don't have to, really."

"No worries. To this evening, ciao."

Mahmud left Fadi's office with a big smile plastered on his face. He closed the door, leaned against it, took a deep breath and headed to his own office.

Back home, Samira and Khadija busied themselves about their modest house. They cleaned, they tidied, they prepared dinner. They bathed, they dressed and they waited for the promised visitor to arrive.

Both of them were thunderstruck, however, when they greeted Fadi at the door. All their expectations of hosting a charming guest crumbled. Samira, simply, didn't like the man; there was something disturbing about him. It wasn't his excessive weight or his commonplace attire. It was his eyes, eyes that spoke of a troubled soul. Khadija didn't like him either; the way he looked at her gave her the chills. His eyes seem to reach out and caress her little body as his tongue licked his lips.

Khadija hid behind her mother when Fadi approached her and offered her a present wrapped in a glittery, pink paper. Mahmud snapped at his five-year-old, scolding her for being impolite, "You say 'thank you' when someone offers you a present!"

Fadi interjected, "It's alright, she's only a cute, little babe."

Eventually, they all ended up at the dinner table. Although Fadi complemented Samira on her delicious cooking and teased Khadija whose face was smudged with tomato sauce, the atmosphere remained tense.

After this night, Fadi began turning up, unannounced, at Mahmud's doorstep every other day or so. Then, the visits became a daily routine. With time, Samira and Khadija felt safer around Fadi although both of them still didn't quite like him.

One stormy evening, Fadi stopped by Mahmud's for a cup of tea. Outside, the wind roared and the rain intensified. Bellows of thunder resounded throughout the house. The forked lightning flashed its glow upon all of Beb-El-Tebbeneh,* including Fadi's harsh features. Khadija nuzzled against her mother and buried her face under Samira's armpit.

Fadi was about to leave when Mahmud offered, "Stay here for the night; the roads are flooded; you won't be able to make it to your place.

"No, no, it's okay. I'll drive slowly, don't worry."

"Oh, come-on, we're not going to allow you to venture outside in such bad weather. Are we Samira?"

"You're most welcome to stay the night. Sorry, we don't have a guest-room," said Samira, "but, believe me, the sofa is comfortable enough."

"All right," said Fadi, "I'll stay since you both insist."

In no time, Samira had spread sheets on the couch and handed Fadi a pillow and a warm blanket. Khadija was already sound asleep on the living room carpet.

Fadi was mesmerized by the child's frail frame. He resisted the urge to hold her in his arms, cuddle her, caress her, kiss her, and make her his. She was exquisite.

Mahmud's eyes met Fadi's and, in that glance, sealed a business deal without uttering one single word. The counterfeit father lifted his daughter into his arms, deposited her in her bed, tucked her in, and studied her awhile before he retreated to his quarters.

Silence and darkness engulfed the house. Fadi stared at the ceiling while his ears were alert to every single sound. When he was finally certain that everyone else was in deep slumber, he pushed the thick throw away, put on the slippers left by Samira next to the divan and advanced towards Khadija's sanctuary. Once there, he peeped through the slightly-opened door.

An anticipation never before experienced took hold of his senses. Desire surged through his blood vessels. Lust seized his whole being. He stood by Khadija's bed watching her angelic face for a few seconds, and, then, he crept in and settled next to her. The child, thinking he was her mother, threw her arms around him but once her hand came into contact with his bearded chin she opened her eyes in alarm and was about to scream when he softly murmured, "My dearest Khadija, I was freezing out there on that sofa so I thought you can help Uncle Fadi regain his warmth." Khadija shifted to the left side of the bed, making space for "Uncle Fadi" who squeezed his large body next to hers.

The girl immediately fell asleep once again. Fadi placed a soft pillow behind his neck and monitored Khadija's every breath and movement. Her flawless, velvety skin reflected the lightning's blaze every now and then. Her delicate neck revealed a gold chain from which dangled a small Koran. Her golden arms hugged a dark, brown teddy bear wearing a red sweater. But it was her tiny, silky legs that made him quiver with pleasure.

Fadi felt his heart race in wild spasms. His blood rushed through his veins like the torrents of rain that were flooding the old city of Tripoli. His yearning was intense. It kept on swelling until it altered into a craving.

Fadi could not withhold his desire any longer. He held Khadija between his stout arms and rocked her until she lost consciousness.

The next day, Samira couldn't figure out Mahmud's unusual happiness, or understand the words her feverish daughter kept repeating, "Uncle Fadi peed on my nightgown! Uncle Fadi peed on my nightgown! Uncle Fadi peed on my nightgown!"

3

GRANDMOTHER, DAUGHTER, GRANDDAUGHTER

Darkness engulfed the one-bedroom house. A foul smell crept into the noses of its inhabitants and reached down into their inner souls, waking up deep, buried instincts. In the left corner, a huge body, in a profound sleep, emanated heavy and regular snores. Other creatures, sharing the sleeping space with the immobile mass, turned this way and that as if dancing to the rhythmic, sonorous music that filled the room.

A frail figure, lying next to the large man, trembled with each heavy breath of her husband. Long, dark hair covered her face. Her feeble arms hugged her tiny breasts as if to protect them from some unknown and undesired invasion. The woman's torn nightgown barely covered her bruised body. She sought warmth and shelter for her feeble legs but the flimsy, stained sheet kept on escaping her cold feet.

But Salma wasn't sleeping. She was waiting. While her body did not betray movement, her whole system was agitated. Her eyelids fluttered as her eyeballs swam fretfully in the darkness.

In the right-hand corner of the chamber, another delicate, even tinier, shape, belonging to a twelve-year-old girl, also was not sleeping. Layal's slender frame rested on a torn mattress, her light, brown hair overflowing onto the hard, icy floor. But, her eyes stared at the ceiling where her young dreams galloped away from her.

Layal's trembling hands crept to her tummy, found the rounded belly and caressed its smooth surface. Then, they retreated, as if ashamed, to lie down next to Layal's body. Layal was being split in two. One part wanted to recognize the woman she had become. The other part clung to the little girl she still wanted to be. Through the darkness, her eyes sought the doll she had dropped next to the wall, by the side of her old pallet a few weeks before. Where did it disappear to?

She missed little Miss Dolly. She needed to hug Miss Dolly and talk to Miss Dolly, the only one who listened to her. It was true that one of Miss Dolly's eyes was missing, and that one of her arms dangled weirdly by her side, but this was Miss Dolly—Layal's loyal and tight-lipped friend. And Layal wanted to tell her a secret, a secret only Miss Dolly could keep.

Layal's hands were now sliding along the cold floor, hunting for what their mistress needed. At last, Layal's hands felt the familiar contours of the doll, and, this time, they came back to Layal proud and victorious. They held Miss Dolly close to Layal's chest and Miss Dolly shushed Layal's hungry stomach, closed Layal's tired eyes, and tucked Layal to sleep.

There was one other person in the room. An old woman crouched in the dark…watching. Her eyes pierced the gloominess of the space. She searched her pockets for a cigarette and found one. She squeezed it between two fingers, brought it to her lips and then slowly chewed it, enjoying the bittersweet taste of the tobacco. She leaned her back against the wall, stretched her legs and sat up on the small, red carpet. She reached for the string that held her thin white hair together, removed it, and shook her head.

Karima waited in her corner while Salma remained motionless and Layal slept. She needed to quench her thirst. Her cold, wrinkled skin longed for the touch of Said's warm, young skin. Her skeletal frame yearned to embrace his robust mass. Her whole being screamed out to him, her son in law. Said opened his eyes, as if he heard the screaming, and looked straight at Karima. He crawled on all fours until he reached her. Half asleep, he approached her and eased himself onto the scarlet rug. He touched her, as if still in a dream, and his touch sent electric currents throughout her dry body, awakening long-forgotten sensations. She welcomed him in hungry defiance of the other two females in the room. Tonight, she, the old matron, would win the heart of the young male.

Salma felt a rush of heat engulf her. She knew this was coming. Although this had often happened in her years of marriage to Said, she still felt this way whenever it did. Salma squeezed her eyes tight, hid them with both hands and rubbed them savagely, as if trying to rip them out. Her hands moved to her ears to block the freaky sounds she was hearing but it was to no avail; the weird noises succeeded in ravaging her inner core. Her heartbeats rushed faster and faster. Cold sweat dripped all over her slender body and waves of laughter shook her soul. Her body began to roll from one side to the other. Her hands were all over her body, stroking it, massaging it, and even beating it in order to calm it down. Salma felt that she had to leave this place…now! She needed fresh air; she needed to breath but her hands couldn't stop beating her body. Her hands couldn't stop beating Said. Her hands couldn't stop beating Karima, her own mother, until a shriek from Layal interrupted everything.

Salma ran to her daughter's side but her mother was already there and shoved her away with such fierceness that she stumbled over Miss Dolly and fell to the floor. By the time Salma was back on her feet, Karima had rushed Layal into the bathroom and locked the door.

Night after night, Karima had been chewing over the thought of another female invading her territory. She had planned for this event and she was more than ready when it finally arrived.

Layal's water broke, running down her legs to the tile floor. Karima shoved her against the broken tiles, forced open her feeble legs, and stuffed her mouth with the dirty piece of hand cloth that was always lying about the smudged tub. Every time the youngster squirmed with a contraction, Karima tightened her grip. Layal's tiny figure twisted and wriggled until an even smaller, more fragile being made an appearance. By the time the tiny baby could breathe it was stopped from doing so and both the twelve-year-old mother and five-minute-old daughter were left inert on the bathroom floor while Karima, the matriarch, inhaled the breath of victory.

On the other side of the door, Salma hugged Miss Dolly in a tight embrace. Said listened, in wonderment, to her lullaby:

> *"Sleep my baby, sleep my puppy*
> *Hold on tight to your Miss Dolly*
> *She will keep you company*
> *Miss Dolly will ride with you up high*
> *Miss Dolly will bake you your favorite pie*
> *Miss Dolly won't make you cry*
> *Hold on tight to your Miss Dolly*
> *She will keep you company."*

4

DAUGHTERS' TRADE

"Hey, you! Young man, talk to me! Hey, listen…yes, you…how about you give me ten thousand Lebanese pounds and I'll allow my daughter to entertain you tonight?"

"Huh, what did you say?" the youth answered, dumbfounded.

Not knowing what to say, he tried to dismiss the old man but the latter wouldn't quit. He kept right on walking by his side and the graybeard continued, "Listen, my daughter is quite an expert; you'll never regret meeting her, believe me. You'll even come back for her!"

It was the holy month of Ramadan.* The streets of Tripoli, glowing with bright lights, were crowded with people. All thoroughfares, alleys, backstreets, corniches and paths…and even dead ends…were illuminated. Colored bulbs dangled from streetlamps and lightened dark corners. Strings of light clinched and curled around lamp posts. Lanterns decorated balconies and swayed with the breeze. Glittering paper moons and stars adorned the shops. After Iftar* and Taraweeh* prayers, the families of the old city invaded the roads in search of gifts, clothes, shoes, and food while its youth filled every coffee shop, deli and restaurant.

Entire families squeezed into tiny boutiques to purchase all sorts of outfits for the coming feast—Eid El Fitr. Fathers conferred at the doorstep of every store discussing politics, sharing points of view. Sometimes they argued. Sometimes they saw eye to eye. Sometimes their exchanges reached a loud crescendo which would only subside when one of the participants caught the stony, disapproving stare of his wife.

In the shops, mothers helped their children try on an assortment of clothes. Shirts flew in the air. Pants landed on top of the heads of customers. T-shirts got passed around hand to hand. Shorts were scattered on the floor and dresses hung askew on hooks. Skirts cluttered every possible space while shoes and socks mixed and mingled everywhere.

Meanwhile, teenagers crammed the cafes to smoke the hubble-bubble and enjoy the famous kaakeh,* stuffed with cheese or thyme. The guys routinely grouped on one side of the coffee shops, ensuring both a view of the girls who walked in as well as of the large TV screens affixed to a wall near the snack bar. The TVs were, usually, tuned to a football game. The young ladies assembled in corners facing the boys. They gossiped. They giggled. And, sometimes, they glanced sideways at the boys, just often enough to encourage their bold advances.

Salima watched the entire hubbub from her chamber window. She wore a flimsy, red nightgown as she knelt on the black couch placed under the wide opening. Her arms leaned upon the windowsill. Her lovely head rested on her soft hands. Tears rolled down her cheeks but her tongue apprehended the salty water before it stained her nightie.

Nearby, her elder sister, Mira, was lying on her bed. She could barely keep her eyes open. As soon as they closed, she fell into a deep sleep and her heavy breathing pulled Salima's attention away from her post. She refocused on the center of the room where the exhausted Mira was stretched out. Although Mira's delicate features seemed tranquil, Salima was well aware that her sister's slumber was a turbulent one.

The door to the girls' boudoir squeaked open, and a stunning brunette appeared. Majida treaded softly into the safe haven and deposited her lovely self next to her sister on the dark settee, under the window.

Salima noticed the streaked face. Without a word, she drew her youngest sibling into her arms, pulled her head against her shoulder, and stroked her long, soft hair. Their slender bodies shook with choked sobs. Majida held tight to her elder and rocked her back and forth in an attempt to alleviate their shared pain.

The weeping pulled Mira out of her nap. She joined the twosome, and the three of them tried to find some comfort in a group hug. For a moment, they stared at each other in silence. Then, they all turned their bodies around to view the street, all resting their elbows on the windowsill.

The three, striking women released their souls, which allowed them to drift along with the Tripolians in the old souks. Their thoughts invaded the shops, penetrated the cafes, investigated the restaurants, crept into the delis, sneaked into sweet shops and even infiltrated the privacy of homes.

Mira's large, brown eyes followed a young, attractive man. He was tanned and muscular. His curly, black hair bounced up and down with every step he took. He was wearing light-blue jeans that hugged his well-developed thighs and a white slim-fit top that embraced his torso. She wondered if he had a sweetheart. She imagined his tender touch, his comforting voice. She envisioned his house, especially his bedroom—the romantic setting where all emotions and passions were spilled. She struggled to dream about love and falling in love. Would she ever experience that weird feeling everybody talked about? She doubted it for how could she understand such a mysterious emotion, particularly if it was related to sex? Wasn't sex pure business as her father had taught her? Weren't sex and money related? Could a person actually enjoy having a sexual relationship?

Salima caught a glimpse of a man in his fifties who was waiting in a long queue at the bakery. She stalked him with her eyes, curious to discover what a true father could offer his family. He was of medium height and wore grey trousers and a blue shirt. In his right hand, he held a clear, plastic bag through which Salima could see fresh buns while in his left hand he clutched a box of maamoul, the famous pastry baked especially for the occasion of Eid el Fitr.

Eventually, the man reached the counter clerk, paid for his purchases and stepped out of the bakeshop. He walked toward a grey Nissan where his wife and kids were waiting for him. The moment he climbed into the vehicle, a flurry of small arms appeared and little hands snatched the bag and the box. Salima could, almost, hear the children laugh and tease each other. She could imagine them stuff first the bread rolls and then the maamoul into their keen mouths. She did notice the parents looking with tenderness at each other and smiling at their kids' voracity. Why couldn't she, Salima, be born into a normal family? Why couldn't she have had a father who sought to protect her? Why couldn't she go to school? Why couldn't her father care about her, or her sisters? Why couldn't they have maamoul?

Next to Salima, Majida bent over the windowsill and focused on two teenage girls who were coming out of a boutique and holding a number of shopping bags. Both of them were tall and slim and wearing trendy outfits. They seemed excited and happy as they walked down the street blabbering, laughing, and bouncing on their feet. A few minutes later, they entered a shoe shop directly across from Majida so she could follow their activities. The two young women wandered around the store inspecting the displayed shoes and bags. They hesitated at some point when one of them grasped a pair of high-heeled red shoes and the other seized an elegant red handbag. They eyed each other, grinned, and, apparently, asked one of the assistants to fetch them the right size of shoes. Without her noticing, Majida's lips drooped, her shoulders sagged, and her heart bled. These two were having the time of their lives. Why couldn't she, Majida, enjoy her teens just like everybody else? Why couldn't she go shopping? Why didn't she have friends? Why couldn't she go out for a movie or a cup of coffee?

Then, the eyes of Mira, Salima, and Majida all shifted to monitor another man's actions. The man who changed, controlled, and manipulated their destiny.

Their father was posted in a shadowy spot, leaning against a stained wall and smoking a cigarette held between darkened fingers. His daughters felt their cheeks burn with shame as they laid eyes on his shabby appearance which never failed to turn their stomachs. His hair was untidy and greasy and his beard long and tangled. He wore a torn, blemished shirt. His tarnished pants hung loose and his sneakers were torn and muddied.

They saw their father leap in front of a young passerby. They knew he was making the young man the same offer he made strange men every night and for the past five years. The sisters watched the man reject their father's offer, as if appalled, and try to dismiss him but, of course, their old man persisted, as usual. He ran after the young male until he spotted another target.

"Hey sir!" he shouted; "Dear sir, I only need ten thousand liras to buy a pack of cigarettes. Oh, oh, don't misunderstand me. I don't want that for free. I have three beautiful daughters, and you can pick and choose. How about that? Ten thousand isn't much to ask for, is it?" They saw the old man, who was his target, stop to talk and, then, shake hands with Malek.

The three girls turned from the window and, in silence, each asked herself …whose turn was it tonight?

5

SISTERS

The mourning sisters held each other tightly and rocked back and forth trying to soothe their mutual pain. Their mother had passed away, in her sleep, that very morning. The deceased's large bed swayed to Maha's and Farah's dance of agony. They buried their faces in the spotless white sheets to breathe in their Mom's perfume. On the night table, the picture of an angelic, middle-aged woman smiled back at them. Maha picked up the golden frame and stared back at the face that was a mix of hers and her sister's. The large brown eyes and the straight nose were definitely hers. The full lips and high cheekbones, they belonged to her baby sister.

Although, this beautiful woman had disappeared forever, her warm voice still echoed in her chamber. "Never forget that blood is thicker than water," she always told her daughters. "Maha! You are strong and seem to be the one who is going to wear the pants in our family!"

Farah, seeking comfort, snuggled against her elder

sister. Maha tapped on her shoulder and offered, "You know, my dear, you're going to feel so lonely in that huge apartment after she's gone, so, Jad and I have decided to ask you to stay with us, and, before you say anything, we won't take no for an answer." The younger woman hugged her sibling closely and breathed in her ear, "Thank you sis, I owe you guys."

Later, Maha made sure Farah was comfortable enough in her new quarters before she retreated into hers. Jad was already in bed. His wife squeezed in beside him. There was no place for words tonight; the couple embraced and drifted to sleep.

But slumber escaped Farah and chaotic memories tripped and tumbled across the room. Farah pushed off the heavy blanket and slipped out of her bed. Tiptoeing, she went to the kitchen, opened the refrigerator, poured a glass of milk, placed herself on a stool, and slowly sipped her drink, now mixed with salty tears. On her way back to her refuge, she stopped by Maha's bedroom; she couldn't help but eavesdrop on the inseparable twosome. The only noise she could make out was heavy breathing. Farah felt jealousy sting her like a wasp. Horrified, she shook her head in negation and proceeded, with haste, to her bedroom.

Farah was shaking violently by the time she slid back under her quilt. "What are you thinking of Farah? For God's sake, Maha is your sister, after all. You couldn't be jealous of your sister; that's pure nonsense! Yet, let's face it Farah, you need a man to comfort you and take care of you. You are thirty-two years old and still alone. But why think of Jad, your sister's husband? Why does it have to be him? You're just in love with him, ever since you laid eyes on him for the first time. You're crazy, Farah, crazy, but I know you pretty well; you've always been one insane woman."

In the morning, Farah joined Maha and Jad for breakfast. When Maha saw Farah's see-through negligee, she dropped her cup of coffee, spilling the hot drink in her lap. Maha jumped out of her chair while Farah ran to her assistance. Maha pushed her sister aside and ran to the bathroom. She undressed and stood under the shower, "Come-on this is your baby sister, and most probably she didn't do it on purpose. She must've thought she was still in the old apartment with your mother or else she wouldn't have dared step out of her room wearing such a revealing gown. Listen, Maha, don't be such a fool. Don't doubt your own flesh and blood; she surely forgot that Jad was in the house."

In the kitchen, Farah attended to Jad's needs. She poured him another cup of coffee, handed him the newspaper, gave him his reading glasses. She, then, positioned herself behind him and started massaging his shoulders.

At first, when Jad became aware of Farah's apparel, he blushed, and felt a surge of desire ravage his senses. Now, he couldn't hide his longing anymore. Farah's hands slipped along his chest, stroked his tummy, and, then, settled once more on his shoulders.

Farah moved away from her brother-in-law, sensually

swaying her hips so he could have a better view. Jad raised his eyes from his newspaper and took a peek at the woman standing in front of him. He put the broadsheet on the table, leaned back in his chair, crossed his legs and observed her more closely. She wasn't what you would call "pretty" but she, surely, was sexy. She was almost naked under that flimsy gown. Her tall, firm legs ended up in a well-rounded curve. Her slim waist bridged her medium-size bosom to her lower body. Her long neck pushed upward, separating from her delicate shoulders, in an attractive way.

Maha stormed into the kitchen, interrupting Jad's scrutiny, and, immediately addressed her husband, "Aren't you running late for work, dear?" Jad pushed his chair back, kissed Maha on her cheek and said goodbye to Farah.

Without saying one word, Maha washed the dishes, fixed the beds, swept the dust, cleaned the bathrooms, and went back to the kitchen to prepare lunch. All the while, Maha couldn't stop thinking about Farah. She kept on grumbling to herself, "Her behavior is really weird. She seems not to have noticed her indecent appearance this morning, most probably, due to her loss. Farah was really attached to our mother and she must feel very lonely. But still that doesn't explain it all, Maha. Don't be stupid! Keep your eyes open for once! Be selfish for once in your lifetime!"

Maha attacked the carrots. She peeled, chopped and washed them. She opened the freezer, removed the meat, threw it in a pot, added water, the necessary salt and pepper, and, then, started the fire. Maha rushed back to the kitchen counter, picked up the sliced carrots, added them to the previous ingredients and attended to the fresh, green peas. The little, round vegetables popped out of their pods and jumped into a casserole. Done with the peas, Maha progressed to the tomatoes. She removed their skins with a sharp knife, hurled them into the food processor, switched on the machine, and pulverized them. She pounded a clove of garlic and minced some parsley. Peas, tomato pulp, garlic, and parsley were drowned in the now boiling water to mix and merge with the stew's previous components. At that moment, Maha took a break and reflected on the previous day's events. "What if," she asked herself, "she had no one to turn to, no degree, no job, no property, no bank account…nothing?"

Leaving her sister by herself to take care of the household chores, Farah ruminated on the early morning's incident. She felt a bit guilty when Maha crossed her mind but she was totally content when she remembered the look on Jad's face. It was about time she made her move. She loved the man and she should stand up for her love, even though her sister was involved. Maha had been married to Jad for twelve years now and had given birth to a girl and a boy. "That's pretty fair," Farah thought to herself, "Now, it's my turn."

She looked in the mirror and assessed her body. It was still firm and tan. Satisfied, she stepped into the bathroom and filled the bathtub with hot water. She dropped her negligee to the floor, settled into the tub and planned her next move. A cunning smile appeared on her face. Her eyes sparkled with a shrewd knowing and she beat the foamy water with her feet in happiness. Farah rinsed her long, thick hair, scrubbed her shining skin, and shaved her well-shaped legs. When she was moisturizing the callous bottom of her heels, she wondered to herself, "What if I could have a man to cherish me, to provide for me, to look after me? A man…for better or worse."

When Jad left the house, the only thing he could think of was Farah's body. He had to have her. He had stopped loving Maha a long time ago; the woman was boring. She cooked, she cleaned, she rubbed floors, and she ironed but he couldn't handle her neglect anymore. She never had time anymore to watch TV with him or give him a massage after a long, rough day at the office. She was always busy tending to the children's needs and never his and in bed she was either tired, or sleepy. Although Maha was still a pretty woman, he couldn't carry on with their relationship any longer.

When Jad stepped inside his office, he ordered his secretary to cancel all his appointments. He sat behind his mahogany desk, loosened his tie, and stretched his legs out on the desk. Tonight, he will solve all his problems, or, actually, his one problem–Maha. He would ask her to leave. He owed her nothing and, deep down in his heart, he felt that Farah would encourage his decision. He knew lust when he saw it and lust was clouding her dark eyes that very morning. "What if?" he breathed heavily. He would experience those exciting moments again. He would regain his youth. He would return home to a sexy woman, a woman who was, apparently, in love with him.

Ten years later, a young man appeared at Jad's doorstep. He handed Jad a package and left. Jad closed the door and looked at Farah with a question on his face. She shook her head; she knew nothing about the bundle. Jad untied the package in a deliberate manner to find two picture frames in his hands. One surrounded a photo of his daughter, the other of his son. The package also contained a golden chain, a candle and a letter. He unfolded the letter and read aloud:

"If you are holding this paper in your hands and reading it with your composed, business-like voice, this means that I am now dead and buried. I just wanted to tell my children how much I loved them and that I always carried them in my heart. By the way, Farah, I forgive you. After all, you were always my little sister and, as Mom used to say, the family pants were mine to wear. As for you, Jad, the father of my children, I would like you to know that I managed on my own. True, I lived in a shack in Beb el Tebbeneh for the past ten years but I found a job as a cook and I coped pretty well. Please tell the children that they can be proud of their mother for how she handled herself. By the way, the gold chain is everything I own and I would like our daughter to have it."

Maha,
Tripoli, Lebanon, 2008

6

THE SEPULCHER

In 2003, during the holy month of Ramadan, in a destitute area located in the midst of a graveyard, in Tripoli, north Lebanon, my friends and I came across an old matron who asked us to provide her with some provisions due to her miserable situation. When we entered her house to fill in a few forms, we came face to face with a 21-year-old man who was completely naked. The woman pleaded, "This is my son, and he is insane." Later, when we stepped outside her residence, we found every single person in her neighborhood standing outside her doorstep. The whole neighborhood screamed at us "Don't believe anything this woman says! She has been raping and drugging her son since he was twelve years old!" Incredulous, I stared back at the woman who simply uttered, "Well, he is mine! I have a right to him! I am entitled to him more than any other woman!"

A seemingly never-ending set of steps links the lower block of the Al Kabr* district to its upper block. On this flight of stairs, hundreds of people mingle and circulate every day. Narrow, long alleys diverge in all directions from the stairway. On one side of those impasses, a number of shabby, tattered shacks lay while on the other side rests an array of tombs. Swarms of people pop out of every corner, every shed, and every single step of the stairway. Children of all ages, some of them barefoot, others half naked, and most of them smudged with dirt, go in and out of the tatty hovels. Kids scatter in every single path. They fill the alleys. They stream up and down the stairway, bumping into whomever or whatever obstructs their way, carelessly knocking down other youngsters. They curse their fate, damn their parents, spit out words of anger and stutter all sorts of insults.

Meanwhile, their mothers position themselves in all corners of Al Kabr* exchanging tittle-tattle and spreading rumors that travel up and down the stairs, even infiltrating the nearby graves, stealing the peace from the dead.

"Hey Fatima! Did you know that Mariam went to visit her parents?"

"Yes, I heard. They say she is going to stay there for a few days."

"Hello Samira! Mariam is staying at her parents because she had a fight with her husband."

"No, no, her mother is sick."

"No, no, no, how can her mother be sick? She took her baby with her!"

"Didn't you hear the news? Apparently, her husband beat her to death yesterday."

"Oh, come on, Umm* Mahmud! Don't exaggerate, he only slapped her."

"Well, she deserves it. This woman can easily hit a nerve!"

"Umm* George! Umm* George, Mariam is getting divorced!"

"To hell with that woman! I always knew she wasn't fit to be a housewife. Isn't that so Umm* Anwar?"

"I totally agree! Since this woman moved to our neighborhood she's led most of our men by their noses. Speak of the devil. Hey, Mariam, where were you?"

"Good morning, ladies! My husband and I took the baby to the pediatrician for his first vaccine."

The women remain faithful to this social duty over the years as if they believe that they cannot survive unless they feed on scandal. Old and middle-aged men totally ignore their claims, as well as their presence, and befriend the arguileh* and its nabrije*.

This daily routine is interrupted only when outsiders arrive. These benevolent visitors pose for a while at the bottom of the staircase to watch the hurly-burly before venturing into the huge, bustling sepulcher. They push their way up the steps, unnoticed at first, but once spotted and identified as strangers or visitors; the inhabitants of Al Kabr* rush and surround them, impeding their progression. Some kids stretch out their hands begging for pennies while others ask for candy and chocolate bars. Some children plead for toys, others for warm clothes. Some shout for Coca-Colas and Pepsi's while more yell for ice-cream and sweets. Adolescents hover close by, requesting fashionable clothes, especially jeans. Mothers cling to their arms soliciting food, most often, milk. Men follow in the footsteps of their children and wives, grabbing the intruders, requesting cigarettes and asking for jobs. Old, tired men drag their feet and attempt to grasp imaginary bottles of whisky while old women supplicate for decent shelter.

The buzz increases until a phantom emerges from out of nowhere and forces Al Kabr* into stillness for a few seconds. People hurriedly disperse in all directions clearing the way for an old mysterious woman, probably in her sixties, her hair as white as snow. Her face is as wrinkled as a crumpled piece of paper, her skin as dry as a thirsty piece of land. Her eyes are sharp and piercing and her mouth is wide and broad as if slit open by a sharp knife. She wears a long, colorless dress, as if time devoured its dye, and wraps a white torn shawl around her shoulders. In short, she seems to be back from the dead. Her presence haunts the tremendous vault. Everybody rushes about seeking a hiding place as if the devil is at their heels. A few minutes later, the bizarre matron disappears inside a small, detached house.

The tiny shack is in a pitiful state. Large fissures violate its walls while shrubs nestle in small holes that encircle the two barred windows. Thorns cover the door's discolored and cracked wood. Spider webs occupy all the corners of the house which consists of two rooms, or actually one, divided by a wooden plank. One space serves as a kitchen and the other as a bedroom. In the first section of the hut, a small refrigerator is placed in the right-hand corner of the room while opposite, on the left, sits a stove. Both domestic appliances seem to be falling apart. In the center of the room, a dirty sink possesses two filthy plates and a pot. On its right, a chair leans its back against the smudged wall. The scullery appears to yearn for its cook— for the woman or the man who will bring back to it the long-forgotten warmth and delicious scents of cookery.

In the other part of the lodge, where a furtive figure moves incessantly, the reeking, excruciating odor of human excrement ravishes the chamber. The form floats around the room. It stops to hover over some neglected bundle placed on some sort of mattress forgotten in the middle of the grimy sleeping quarters. It kneels next to a scrawny human being, extends her hands and rubs his chest. The male grabs the female. A hoarse groan is heard followed by heavy breathing. The shadow of two peculiarly intermingled bodies stretches against the room's yellow wall. Al Kabr* resounds with the squeaks of a bed, the swoosh of caresses, and the rustle of sheets.

The echo of incomprehensible murmurs reverberates in every single house and resonates in every single heart, traumatizing the residents of Al Kabr.* Later, the whispers will turn into savage shrieks and a spectral silhouette rises and shakes its bones.

The ghostly figure of a nude, bearded, young man appears behind the bars of a dimly-lit window. His long hair, falling over his face in chaotic fashion, covers most of his features. His lifeless eyes stare into the darkness as if searching for a spark of hope. His hands grip the iron bars with fierceness as if attempting to bend them so that he can flee the miserable hut. Although his emaciated legs seem to quiver under his slight body weight, they long to run and jump freely around the streets. His muscles tremble whenever a slight breeze touches them. His whole being screams incessantly for a long-sought freedom but behind him an overwhelming apparition obstructs his thoughts, feelings and movements.

She glances at Al Kabr*'s dark alleys, smiles mockingly, approaches the wild man, strokes his unkempt hair, and then explores every inch of his bare body with her creased hands. She purrs, pouring all her venom into his soul. She ensnares the young male's spirit in an eternal embrace where mother and son remain motionless. The first gazes intently at the graveyard while the latter fastens his eyelids shut in an attempt to withhold his tears.

7

A BEAUTIFUL FACE

"I saw your sister having a close conversation with Maher yesterday. They were standing in a corner, next to Abu* Youssuf's grocery store. Hey! I am talking to you, Khalid. Did you hear what I said? Your sister Dima was…"

"Yes, yes, I heard you."

Khalid dragged his bulky mass down the street, while his so-called best friend, Mazin, kept on blabbering about Dima's beauty, and how her brother should protect her against all evil. Khalid, becoming agitated, strode towards Abu Hamza's humble house where he found the old, sly man leaning over his fence.

"Good morning, Khalid! Why are you frowning? Is anything wrong?"

"Salam,* Abu Hamza! No nothing is wrong. Everything is fine, don't worry."

"By the way, I heard that Dima is going to attend the American University of Beirut this coming fall to pursue her studies, and I also heard that your respected father agreed to send her to the lion's den."

"Yes, true.

"Listen, my boy, you know perfectly well that Beirut is the household of evil and Dima is a beautiful young woman. Therefore, it is your duty to make sure she doesn't dice with death.

"Yes, yes, I know."

Khalid knitted his brow and marched to Tripoli's flea market. When the souk's hubbub reached his ears, it added to the commotion of thought that was commuting back and forth between his mind and his heart.

Merchants were screaming. Abu Ali stood next to his booth waving a blue scarf, trying to attract women to his silky merchandise. Abu Fadi had positioned himself on a stool and was honking a klaxon; its sonorous sound led people to his colorful stand of used shoes. Hisham quietly ushered the souk's visitors into his tiny cubicle where bits and pieces of wooden carvings crammed messily. On a kitchen table covered with a blue cloth, Miriam was placing an assortment of pots, a few glasses, a number of tea mugs and several Turkish coffee cups. She was holding one of the pots in her hand and hitting it hard with the other to promote her goods. On a torn carpet, Tarik displayed some running shoes, a few socks, and many flip-flops. Abu Muhammad sat in a shady spot on the sidewalk arranging differently-sized rolls of tobacco leaves inside a wooden box. Next to him, Um* Muhammad was relaxing in a dilapidated armchair while smoking a cigarillo and stroking her skeletal cat.

Noha, a tall, attractive woman, sold homemade products. On her long, narrow table, bottles of rose water, pomegranate juice, apple cider, strawberry juice, and olive oil leaned intimately against each other. Yasser, a teenager, wandered the flea market, clicking his coffee cups together in an attempt to persuade passers-by to take a break and enjoy some of his "Turkish mystical warm drink." Unfortunately, for him, most of the market's visitors preferred to take a breather by the Andalusian* fountain which divided the bazaar into two distinct areas.

On the other side of the small pool, Um* Ibrahim settled down on a ripped red sofa placed by her sukkah. She didn't make any effort to invite customers into her tattered booth. She just sat there smoking the arguileh* while her faithful dog hid under her settee, licking her heels and watching the on-going hullabaloo of the souk.

Khalid, upon reaching Um* Ibrahim's zone, stopped for a moment. He assessed her from head to toe with disgust and then moved on while muttering, "A woman should better bury herself alive after her husband's death."

Finally, he reached Wissam's stand, where he grabbed a chair, sat down, and lit a cigarette. Wissam greeted him with a snarl and continued carving the piece of wood he carefully held between his fingers.

Khalid leaned forward and asked his friend, "Have you seen Dima today?"

"I wish!"

"What do you mean...you wish?"

"Oh! For God's sake, as if you didn't know that all men in this town wish to lay their eyes on your sister's exquisite face and body every single minute of the day!"

Khalid scowled and continued on his mission.

"Hey man! I was kidding," shouted Wissam after him, but Khalid stormed into Abu Issam's stall where shirts of every color and size were neatly folded.

"Hala ya hala,* Khaled, how are you doing?"

"Fine, how was your day?"

"El-hamdulillah,* sold a few for some tourists. How is your family, especially your gorgeous sister?"

"O.K., I guess."

"I saw her a while ago. She was with Shafika."

"Shafika?"

"Yeah, you know Shafika, Shoushou, the Beiruti girl."

"Yes, yes, now I remember her!"

"Have you seen Shoushou lately?"

"Nope."

"You'd better! I mean woo, man! She's hot and she doesn't hide it...on the contrary, ouf!"

"What do you mean?"

"She wears those very short, tight skirts in such a way that it makes one think about what's hidden underneath. And, my God, her breasts! I've never laid eyes on anything like those two before!

"That's not good news at all!"

"For your sister... hmm, not at all! Better beware!"

Khalid's head buzzed with all sorts of questions. "What if Dima was following in the footsteps of Shafika? What if Dima has a boyfriend? What if Dima brought shame upon him and his father? Better deal with the problem before it gets out of hand."

With determined and resolute strides, Khalid made his way back home but Dima was nowhere to be found.

"Mom, Mom, have you seen Dima?"

"Yes dear! Shafika dropped by, and they both left for Beirut a few minutes ago."

Fuming with anger, Khaled stormed out of the house and headed for the bus station.

Dima stared blankly at the passing scenery. Neither the sea nor the green fields succeeded in changing her mood. She shifted her attention to Shoushou who was sound asleep in the seat next to hers. Shafika's head rocked back and forth in perfect synchronization with the bus's swaying movement. Her long, black hair covered most of her angelic face. Dima smiled at her sleeping friend and then her focus shifted to the strange faces that now stared back at her from the other seats.

The passengers seemed serene but something disturbing overshadowed their expressions.

The fat woman sitting on her left hugged a large plastic bag against her chest. Her brown eyes were watery. An ugly spot, black and violet, stained her white cheek. By her side, sat a young lady whose haggard looks made Dima wriggle in her place.

Consequently, Dima's eyes settled on the gaunt face

of a teenager. The young brunette's lips trembled. Actually, her whole body shook. A serene middle-aged man sat next to her and possessively held her fragile hand in his large, coarse paw.

In the front seat sat an old man. He held a rosary in his veined hand and his lips muttered with every bead.

In the back of the bus, a family of four was settled. Actually, the children were all over the place but their parents ignored their comings and goings.

Finally, Dima relocated her interest and her eyes rested upon a young man who held a great resemblance to her brother, Khalid. Gradually, pain and fear invaded her whole being. Numbness assaulted her body and deadness took hold of her lively spirit. Body and soul merged, melted, and vanished with the waves that lightly stroked the chiseled coastline of the capital.

Later, Dima found herself with Shafika treading down the streets of Beirut. They cut through the darkness which was getting thicker by the minute. Dima could barely make her way along the narrow alley that led to Shafika's house. The path was smooth and her feet easily slipped on the asphalt. At one point, she held her arms straight out in front of herself expecting at any moment to bump into something or someone. The obscurity surrounded Shafika's body, embraced it, and concealed it entirely from Dima's field of vision. A cat slipped between Dima's legs sending sensual tremors down the young woman's back. Murmurs and laughter escaped from windows awakening the most primitive desire in the core of her being. Suddenly, Dima felt uncomfortable. She peeked furtively to her left, and then, to her right but she didn't dare look behind for the resounding echo of muffled footsteps was hunting her. She searched the darkness for her friend Shafika but her eyes couldn't pierce the black dress of the night. She was hurrying to reach the safety of her friend's house when a cold, sweaty hand grabbed her by the shoulder, pulled her to a stop and swiveled her violently on her heels. Her heart was pounding as she came face to face with her Honor Guardian.

High above the streets of Beirut, some people were settling down to eat their evening meal, some others were trundling off to bed in their slippers, and a few were almost falling asleep when, from down below, they heard a young woman scream "Khaled!"

8

THE GRID

The Grid wakes up every morning to the Mou'ezen's* prayers. It also wakes up to the squabbling of incompatible couples, the screaming of angry, frustrated teenagers and the cries of hungry children. Listen more closely and you'll also hear the resigned grunts of the sick and elderly, the babbling of ongoing gossip, and the desperate bellows of distressed merchants. You'll hear the barks of famished dogs and the startling cries of starving cats mixed with the impatient beeps of various horns and klaxons. The ding-dongs ringing from beat-up bicycles, the sonorous creak of heavy pushcarts, and the echoing bangs of heavy cases being dropped all add to the symphony.

People of all ages and sizes pour out of disfigured buildings and rush in every direction, every street, every alley, and every corner of The Grid. The area becomes crowded with people running, walking, and creeping. Every type of wheeled vehicle, four-footed animal, and flying and crawling insect make their appearance. Every creature shoves and digs to find itself a space on the cracked and sewage-flooded sidewalks of The Grid, all inhaling the polluted, malodorous air that intoxicates the underprivileged area.

The Grid's shopkeepers open their shop doors with anticipation. Abu* Yussef, the butcher, is always the first to unlock the doors to his shop. Once he sets foot in his store, he positions himself behind the counter and starts barking out orders at his men. "Abdullah! Hurry up! Hurry up! Clean the chicken breasts and place them in the green dishes. Ali! To your duty immediately! You're responsible for the steak; remove all the fat and arrange the meat in the blue platters. Saleem! The chops Saleem, this time they have to be ready before the first customer arrives. Ghassan! Mr. Turtle, move it and assemble the ribs in the yellow salvers."

Abdullah, Ali, Saleem, and Ghassan rush to their chores, one bumping into the two skinned and dangling cows and another colliding with the four pared sheep hanging down from the ceiling.

The scent of raw meat escapes the butcher's shop and mixes with the fragrance of freshly-baked bread. The odor of dried, ferrous blood and the aroma of sweet, crisp bread merge and call to both meat and bread shoppers alike.

Abu Mussa, the baker, is constantly on the go around his bakery. He dashes from one side of the shop to the other, sometimes rearranging the loaves of bread and, ever so often, attending to his clients' needs. The crunchy baguettes stand in large, wicker baskets by the door while the brown bread, wrapped in plastic, is laid out in stretches on a nearby counter. The popular white bread, known as pita, is stacked on long wooden planks awaiting its fans. The buns, brioches, and croissants ensnare passers-by with their delicious odor, demanding that people renounce their diets.

Meanwhile, Abu Khodor dashes around his grocery store, cleaning, sweeping and buffing up his fruits and vegetables. The area is divided into two parts. On the left, sparkling fruits await the caressing hands of buyers while, on the right, messy stacks of vegetables anticipate their countless handlings and assessments. Meanwhile, Abu Khodor is always busy wandering about his shop and, at times, pausing only long enough to deliver a stealthy pinch to his young employee or sneakily shoving him. The lad always tries his best to avoid his employer's aggressive assaults but Abu Khodor's transgressions never fail to catch him when he least expects it.

The fish market, situated in a small parking lot next to Abu Khodor's, welcomes bargain hunters and sells its catches in noisy auctions. Abu Mustapha positions himself on a chair, holding a dripping bag in one hand and a microphone in the other. He starts the auction with ten thousand "Lebanese Liras."* "The catch of the day, ladies and gentlemen," he shouts, "It's fresh, it's clean, and, when fried, crispy and yummy!" He waits a few seconds then screams again, "Come on, fellows, ten thousand, I said. Finally, I have ten thou over there. Oh! Oh! I have twelve thou to the right! Oh! Oh! One minute, I have fourteen thou here, here in front of me. Sold for fourteen thou! Sahteyn,* sahteyn, ya Afandee*!" Abu Ahmad grabs the carrier bag and proceeds to his basketry while Abu Mustapha carries on until every single fish is sold.

Abu Ahmad unlocks the doors to his workshop and immediately heads to the untidy kitchen to prepare his morning coffee. The place is filled with baskets of all sizes, shapes and colors. Bread baskets align shelves. Picnic baskets huddle in the left corner of the shop while wicker baskets pile up opposite. Scattered laundry baskets everywhere hinder the movement of shoppers.

Abu Ahmad's faces the pharmacy where Abu Hassan, the chemist, prepares his herbal medicine. Herbs, dried flowers and grounded spices decorate Abu Hassan's desk where he busies himself every day, combining and mixing ingredients until he comes up with his magical potions. "Good morning Amo,* Abu Hassan!" shouts Layla, the hairdresser. "Good morning, habeebtee*!" answers Abu Hassan who hurries to the door in a clumsy bustle to flirt with the young woman before she opens up her salon. Their chit-chat lasts for five minutes before they both disappear inside their safe havens upon the sight of Abu Waheed, the carpenter.

Abu Waheed draws near his woodworking workshop with seeming nonchalance while he scrutinizes the street with a look that is both curious and chilling. He unbolts the doors to the place where he oversees cabinetmaking, carpentry, carving, joinery, and marquetry. Abu Waheed settles down behind his counter and the kids start arriving one after the other.

Yussef, five years old, seizes the dirty broom and begins mopping the floor. His tiny, blistered fingers cannot even close tightly around the broomstick. His watery eyes cling to the shop's tiles, not missing one single sliver of wood. He drags his feet as he follows his sweeping whooshes.

Mussa, six years old, positions himself by the tool boxes and begins sorting out the awls, the bradawls, the dills, the hammers, the jigsaws, the mallets, the planes, the sanders, the saws, and the vises. Mussa's job is to maintain and secure the tools and his fearful, worried eyes seek out the devices in order to return them to their proper cases. When he's not distributing the instruments to his anxious colleagues or putting them away after use he cleans them with a soft, stained cloth and scrubs them with a rough, torn sponge, all executed with great fussiness.

Khodor and Maher, the seven-year-old twin brothers, sit on stools in the darkest spot of the workshop. Khodor arms himself with a hand plane and pushes the iron tool forward leaving a smooth surface on the piece of wood placed between his knees. Meanwhile, Maher takes hold of the sanding machine and, bending his head low, begins the arduous work of smoothing down surfaces, a task he performs in silence, for hour after hour each and every day.

Mustapha and Ahmad, eight-year-old cousins, seat themselves next to Khodor and Maher. One holds an awl and the other a bradawl. Mustapha marks the pieces of wood with his pointed tool and Ahmad pierces the plank holes in preparation for the work of the joiners, Kareem and Kassem, both ten years old.

Finally, Hassan, fifteen years old, stands behind the vise. He inserts the wooden planks between the machine's jaws and tightly clamps them down.

Abu Waheed observes his crew one at a time. Yussef's little body rises and falls as he follows his broom in rhythmic movement. Watching this synchronized locomotion makes Abu Waheed feel weak at the knees. He coughs, murmurs a few incomprehensible words, and then looks over to Mussa. The latter, full of devotion to his job and always in a hurry, constantly forgets to zip up his pants. Abu Waheed's eyes linger on the opened fastener and its crooked metal teeth, igniting a strong, burning emotion that rocks Abu Waheed back and forth. He shakes his head, adjusts his position on his seat, and turns his gaze to the twins. Khodor and Maher are totally engrossed in polishing and smoothing. The two novices in their shady spot never fail to stir up the weirdest feeling in Abu Waheed's guts. He can barely discern their features yet he can still imagine their full lips and sense their silky and velvety hair under his rough, coarse hands.

Abu Waheed snaps out of his reverie and stares at Mustapha and Ahmad. The cousins were hostile when he first employed them but, now, they cater to his needs without shame. They are, at all times, ready to oblige his whims, for the two little monsters have grown to enjoy it as well. In their presence, he is the man of the moment.

Abu Waheed takes pleasure in his achievement for a few minutes and then watches Kareem and Kassem. Kareem is tall for his age and his slim figure spreads goose bumps along Abu Waheed's aged body. This kid always gives him a hard time. Just the thought of struggling with the boy each time he even comes near him makes the old man groan and snort. As for Kassem, that one is dumb and Abu Waheed cares little about him. He can get hold of him any time he chooses. Finally, his eyes settled on Hassan. His apprentice has grown into a young man, and Abu Waheed doesn't have a taste for men; children are his preference. Consequently, when today's work is finished, he will bid Hassan goodbye and thank him for the good old days.

In the evening, the same turmoil repeats itself in "Beb El Tebbeneh.*"

Abu Yussef and his staff clean the meat shop. One holds the hose and squirts water everywhere. Another shoves the water about with a broom while a third dries the wet surfaces with cotton cloths. A fourth stores the remaining meat in the freezer as Abu Yussef counts the cash in his drawer.

Abu Mussa locks the doors to his bakery and heads to the café at the end of the street. He dumps himself in a chair and orders an arguileh* and a cup of Turkish coffee. Later, Abu Khodor joins him and asks the waiter for a mug of jasmine tea. Both of them wait for the rest of the men to arrive in order to start a game of poker. Once everybody settles down, the booze is passed around and, from mouth to mouth, the bottles are emptied until the last drop. Next, hashish* cigarettes circulate among the drunkards adding to their numbness. The foggy coffee shop buzzes with noise. The gamblers fight and cheat; the drunken men sing along with Fairuz.* The doped ones dance to some tune that only they can hear and the waiters shout orders to the chef.

Then, the evening bustle stops dead the moment that Abu Waheed secures the doors to his workshop confining the children inside for two, maybe three more hours. The men fall completely silent but they listen hard, barely breathing. They sweat profusely as they wait for their sons to show up. They will remain in their places so as to steal a peek at Abu Waheed's face when he leaves his shop for they all agree on one thing— Abu Waheed pays their way.

The boys run around the shop, arrange the tools and clean the area. Then, like a flock of sheep, enter the anteroom, one after another, and close its door. All the youngsters crouch together in the tight room while holding hands, except for Hassan who stands in the middle of Abu Waheed's quarters.

Under the close scrutiny of his boss, the apprentice lazily removes his clothes. First, he sheds his shirt. Next, in a careless gesture, he drops his vest to the floor. After that, he starts at his zipper. It gets stuck and he fights with it until it gives in to his wet hands. He drops his pants, takes a deep breath, and finally, dispenses with his briefs. Hassan closes his eyes, hugs himself, and turns his back.

This time, it is different because he knows it is the last. He recognizes that he has to look for another job starting tomorrow. He realizes that he has to face his father's wrath. He knows that his dad will whip him. He reckons his mother will do all she can to protect him. He imagines that his siblings' loud screams will awaken the neighbors but he is also certain that he will not be at the mercy of Abu Waheed any longer. He will not be at the mercy of The Grid any longer. He will not be held captive by Beb El Tebbeneh any longer.

9

PRICELESS BABIES

Dear Sir/Madam,

I would like to seek your help in a matter that is highly personal and emotional to me. It is a decision that I have not taken lightly. Although I was born in Lebanon, I was adopted and raised in the Netherlands. I hope to interest you and your readers in the story of my adoption. I am seeking publicity so that I can reach out to my biological mother and let her know that I am all right. If she would like to make contact that would, of course, be wonderful. My main purpose, however is to pass on the message to her that things worked out in the end. I should be most grateful if you would see if you can find out any further details, run the story in your paper and pass on any possible responses.

I was born on 6th December 1973. Although the adoption papers state that I was born in Beirut, the agent who arranged for the adoption, Mrs. Adla Chemayel, stated to my adopted parents that I was born in Tripoli, and that my biological mother came from the mountains around Beirut and my biological father owned an orchard. Sadly, she has since denied all the information given earlier and has refused to provide any further details.

I do not know the reason why I was given up for adoption. What I do know is that many mothers in similar situations were persuaded to give up their children, and left penniless, even though the adoption agents themselves made a lot of money out of these transactions. I only recently discovered these agencies' corruption. Having given birth to my first child in 1999 I am convinced that a mother never forgets that experience and that this event coupled with the corruption involved must have caused a lot of pain and sadness. I would like my biological mother to know that, although at times I have struggled to come to terms with my adoption, my life has not altogether been overcome with such sadness, other than, perhaps, the frustration at how she must have been treated at the time.

I would be grateful if you could consider placing an article (perhaps illustrated with a picture?) about my story and assist in letting my biological mother know that I am doing well, and that she has two grandchildren. My story may also comfort the other mothers who were forced to give up their babies – after all, the main message is that despite the hurtful separation of mother and child there can be a happy ending. And last, but not least, I believe that my story will also be of interest to other readers as it is the story of some 300 Lebanese-born babies abroad.

I look forward to hearing from you.
Yours faithfully,
Krista Visser
Date of birth: 6th December 1973
Place of birth: officially Beirut, but in all likelihood, Tripoli
Date of adoption: 26th December 1973
Name: Krista Visser

The shabby, abandoned hospital still squeezed in among the frayed buildings of Syria Street in Beb el Tebbeneh. Layers and layers of sweaty, stinky people covered the streets of this gloomy area of northern Lebanon as if the flotsam and jetsam of the universe was deposited in that baleful neighborhood.

Remnants of human beings dragged their feet along the wrecked sidewalk. Since dawn, they had been wandering the nasty pigsty of roads in search of leftovers. They begged passers-by for coins and they rummaged the filth-coated garbage containers for scraps. They even filched their needy neighbors' petty possessions when they could. By sunset, they had all retreated back to their nearly-demolished homes, leaving the scene to drug dealers, drug addicts, alcoholics, delinquents, and crooks. Although Beb el Tebbeneh bustled with felons, this hadn't stopped Lama from venturing into the place.

In 2009, on one of December's coldestnights, Lama stood in the middle of the frontage that separated the sanatorium from the main street. Upon laying eyes on her birthplace, goose bumps ran along Lama's limbs. Thirty-five years had passed since her mom had given birth to her in that desolate hospital.

The hospice's façade was worn out and grimy. With the years, the white paint, which still covered some of its exterior had transformed into a mousy color. The stripped, grey patches of cement that tarnished the rest of the building enhanced its obscure appearance. And, every night, it seemed, the deserted establishment turned into a shelter for the homeless.

Lama proceeded with a faltering step until she reached the main entrance. She paused for a few moments at the threshold before opening the swinging barrier that separated her from her past.

Entering the large vestibule, Lama was greeted by the sight of the many dispossessed who had flung their bodies upon the icy, gashed marble of the old hospital. She paused to contemplate the atrium. It certainly was filthy. Five doors linked the huge hall to five endless corridors and the deserted reception desk seemed miserable without its occupants. Lama advanced toward the counter and, with her finger, drew a circle on its dusty surface. She was trying to decide which of the five passageways to examine first. She noticed an inscription on the wooden access to the second passageway on her right. She removed her reading glasses from her red shoulder bag and tried to decipher the engraved words. They had been carved with some kind of sharp instrument. But Lama couldn't decipher the message. She drew out a black marker from her bag and started coloring in the carved inscription. "And they surrounded them like a wolf pack scenting an easy prey," she murmured.

Lama felt her heart contract. Her whole being vacillated. With caution, she pushed open the squeaky, swinging door and stepped into the narrow hallway. The sudden, loud creaking of the door closing behind her caused her to jump out of her skin. Lama took a deep breath.

The passage was dark and sinister; she couldn't even perceive its end. In a frenzy, she searched her bag for a lighter and once its flame glowed, piercing the obscurity, she proceeded onward. Lama opened the first door to her left. The room she walked into was lit by a streetlamp shining through a large, grimy window. The place was empty, except for some wires which dangled from the grey walls.

Lama quickly inspected the rest of the rooms. Nothing caught her attention; they were all the same... bare, cold and humid. She kept on opening and closing doors until she reached the middle of the corridor where a large, glass-enclosed space attracted her like a magnet. She stood there mesmerized. This, most likely, was the nursery.

Lama stuck her nose against the grubby window but couldn't perceive anything clearly. She stepped inside what a rusty sign announced was the "intensive care" area. The moist odor of the spacious room hit her in the face. A feeling of déjà vu took hold of her. She felt faint, and her head spun with a surge of memories. She leaned back against one of the walls and gazed at the ceiling where her reflections danced and projected images as old as she was.

Then, she sensed a presence; someone was watching her. In a flash, a hand grabbed her clothing and pulled her down to the floor and Lama found herself face to face with what seemed to be an old nurse. "You are one of them. Aren't you?" the grey face spit out. "You came back here to punish me! You are after me, aren't you?"

Tongue-tied, Lama shook her head in negation. She closed her eyes and listened intently to the woman's ghostly voice which echoed along the pathway. The eerie voice transported Lama back thirty-five years in time, back into the hospice's nursery, back into one of the incubators. The woman took Lama by her hand and they both sneaked inside the babies' room. The old matron held her index finger to her mouth, shushing Lama, as she showed her the empty room.

The old nurse became hysterical and began shouting, broadcasting her hallucinations to Lama, "It's a boy! It's a girl! See the nurses rushing everywhere holding either a pink or a blue bundle in their arms? They're coming to lay their packages in their proper nests. Once the tiny cots are filled, the nurses will hurry to execute their duties, one child at a time. One nurse will wash the baby, a second will dry, a third will take the baby's temperature, a fourth will handle blood pressure, a fifth will dress and wrap, and a sixth will feed and burp. Then, the little creatures will sleep soundly."

The nurse's fingernails penetrate Lama's tender skin as she continues, "Now, see this woman in white circling the area, moving from one crib to the other. She's holding a paper on which numbers are scribbled—6, 10, and 15. Look! She walks among the newborn, scrutinizing the labels attached to each small bed. Wherever she sees a name inscribed, she will turn away and keep searching for the numbers. Now, she is picking up number 6, a reddish, baby boy, and handing him over to that frail, pale man standing in the shadows behind the yellow curtain. Number 6 is gone. Ah! She's found number 10, a baby girl with a bald head and chubby cheeks, and, look, she's handing her to another female nurse. One more to go!"

The old nurse swivels Lama about and continues, "See how swift and agile I am as I seize number 15, and tightly hold the blond baby girl against my chest. This is you! Right? You are screaming, but since crying babies are an on-going event here no one is paying attention to that pale man. See, he's passing you through a window to a woman. There's a blue van parked by the hospital's backdoor, and the three of you and your abductors are roaring away from the scene. Do you hear the engine? …Gone!"

Lama pulled her eyes away from the nurse's lips, and her body from the nurse's grasp, and she moved, alone, along the two rows of rooms. In a trance, she retreated back into the hall. Her sight licked every entrance; her mind questioned every chamber, "Did you embrace my mother? Did you listen to her pain? Did you witness her agony?" Her heart pleaded, "Please dear God, one clue, one clue only. How can I find my mother?"

Lama broke into tears. She sobbed for the parents she never met. She cried for the Christian woman who was her mother. She wept for the Muslim man who was her father. She shed tears for the two lovers who, a long time ago, crossed the threshold of that now ruined hospital, knowing that this was their last time as a family. In those days, a Christian and a Muslim were not allowed to stay together.

Lama lamented her fate as well as the fate of the other 300 Lebanese babies who were sold to Dutch families in 1973.

10

THE ROCKING BED

Mona's eyelids flared open. Her eyeballs darted to and fro within their watery orbits and questions stormed her wide, brown eyes. The only thing she could feel and comprehend was a rocking movement which made her nuptial bed tremble. Her body quavered with the fear of the unknown.

Dread crept into Mona's heart as an alien terror paralyzed her limbs for she couldn't identify the source of her trepidation. She gazed into the impenetrable blackness, trying to remember where she was. She saw only darkness. She couldn't even perceive the borders of the bed. Worse still, she couldn't even visualize the room she shared with her husband or the apartment they had moved into a week before. In a kind of shock, the newlywed tried to recollect her senses in order to understand and assess the sweeping emotions which enclosed her heart, entranced her mind and enfolded her spirit.

With great effort, Mona attempted to pinpoint the origin of the swaying motion that disturbed her peaceful slumber. Without shifting her position, Mona forced herself to develop a mental picture to explain the curious activity that controlled her matrimonial bed. Failing to imagine the cause of her trouble, Mona focused on the sounds of the shadowy dusk. Perhaps her four-poster danced to the explosion of missiles, but, no, the civil war was still raging in her beloved Lebanon but, apparently, tonight, all parties had decided to take a break.

More determined than ever to find out the reason for the uncontrollable tremor, Mona turned her head with a slow and calculated movement. Her eyes found the chandelier staring quietly back at her. It wasn't an earthquake.

Right then, the commotion increased. It escalated gradually into a rapid quivering shudder. A moment later, the pretty bride heard a growing moan originating from the man who lay beside her in the rocking bed. In a panic, Mona turned over in one swift movement to witness a sight she had never even imagined.

The beautiful Mona, craved by all, pursued by most and desired by every eligible bachelor, saw her world crumbling in a heap all around her. Here she was, sleeping next to the man she chose to marry, the man of her dreams, the partner she loved, the father of her future offspring, the husband she was supposed to cherish and honor all her life. And he was now, all of a sudden, a complete stranger.

Her eyes were mesmerized, fixed on the stranger's

hands. The stranger rubbed and rocked, until his semen spluttered on his flat stomach.

"What a waste! What a terrible waste!" muttered Mona between her teeth as she turned her back on the stranger, her mate, her past, her present, and her future.

11

THE MEMBRANE

It was 6 p.m. on a spring evening in a sinister area in North Lebanon. The gynecologist's clinic overflowed with females of all ages, colors, and sizes who gathered and buzzed in the waiting room of black leather chairs and couches. They had all squeezed into this numb room for the same reason. They were all getting married but, first, they all had some business to attend to.

The doctor strolled in and they all rose to greet their savior. He was tall and handsome in his white robe but he seemed heartless. His features were severe, almost cruel. At this time of day, he had to be both nurse and physician and his features betrayed an annoyance that he couldn't hide. He stepped inside his private office and picked up the clipboard which awaited him on the oak desk. The list of names changed every day. After what seemed like a very long time to the waiting women, he called out the first name on the list in a steady, unperturbed voice. A young, brown-haired woman rose up and disappeared behind the office door.

All of a sudden, as if some invisible puppeteer had decided to put them all into motion, the women in the reception area couldn't sit still anymore. One of them got up to march around while biting her fingernails. Another started giggling as if someone had just told her a hilarious joke. A teenager, on a small settee, burst into tears. An eighteen-year-old blond shifted her weight on her seat from hip to hip. A brunette's eyelids began fluttering as if she no longer had control over them while a twenty-eight-year-old was twiddling her thumbs. A plump girl grasped a pencil lying on a coffee table and proceeded to gnaw at it. A mother began a fretful tap on her daughter's purse. An old woman yanked at the hair of a young woman who was clutching her handbag as if she was expecting some thief to snatch it from her.

In the midst of this sudden activity, the flock of females exchanged pitiful looks which related the whole story...the story of honor. None of them spoke, but they all felt the same. They were all trapped. The herd was stuck in the same tiny hole where a previous generation was caught and where the next generation will be jammed into again.

In one quick motion, a dark-haired teenager stood up and left the clinic. Thunderstruck, all the women became silent. Many of them lowered their heads and concentrated on their shoes. An invisible weight pressed them down until they were almost sitting in a bowed position. Their minds spun and whirred. They so wanted to reflect on their situations but no reflection was allowed. Their presence, in that "restoration room," was proof enough of both their physical and spiritual abduction.

The women returned to their frantic activity, many pacing up and down the room, increasing worry with every step. Why was the first patient taking so long?

They all stopped when they heard the door squeak open. Their eyes hung onto the pale face that appeared at the threshold. They monitored it for any expression that could appease their edginess. But all they saw was a look of pain and humiliation.

Convulsions of laughter shook a young brunette who had been silent until now. "Ahh! Hahahaha! Ouh! Ouh! It seems that this tiny membrane, haha, will never loosen its grip! Ouh! Damned and doomed forever! Haha! You all think your problems will end in this clinic! Don't you? Well, listen to me all of you! I said lend me your ears! No love, no equality, and no modernity is gonna come forward and speak up for us! Even rape and incest will not buy our ticket to purity! We are all guilty for being born female. We are nothing but walking vaginas! That's what we are, and nothing will ever change this fact. So, wake up and make your choices, dear sisters! Either you choose to be a creeping vagina or a strutting vagina!"

12

THE FLESHY EXPERIENCE

The young couple stormed into the dimly-lit suite chuckling, flirting, teasing and touching. The aromatic candle flames projected their dancing shadows upon the chamber walls where the phantoms of Aphrodite and Eros merged to perform their own captivating ritual. Crimson roses diffused out of the many dispersed vases, adding to the room's intoxicating scent. Red curtains dropped from the ceiling and enfolded the boudoir's guests in a tender and affectionate embrace. A scarlet divan, no doubt hungry for some soft flesh to caress, rested in one of the murky corners of the bedchamber. The many paintings on the walls observed every single movement while every exotic fruit in the basket sitting on the elegant round table expectantly waited to be kissed. An immense bed, sprinkled with petals and chocolates, seemed to anticipate the fleshy collision against its fresh crispy, sheets.

Meanwhile, the bride and groom's laughter journeyed across the glittering corridors to reach every ear, restoring hearing to the deaf. Their merriment tiptoed out of their chamber, settling on every stern face and turning the gnashing of teeth into enchanted smiles. Their murmurs gave free rein to all repressed emotions. Their passion gushed out of every corner and surged through every beating heart, unleashing its palpitations on a wild forgotten ride. Their love flowed and found its way into every scruffy, rusted brain, triggering entrancing memories. In a crescendo of lights, scents, tastes, visions, sounds, emotions, passion, pleasure, desire, and lust, all swelled up, conspired, and exploded. The resulting array of confused, mixed feelings began to douse their senses, one after the other, until they both fell lifeless on the messy bedroom's floor.

The husband lay on his left side, his eyes closed, fantasizing about his next blast. The wife lay on her right side. Her eyes were open but her mind was hanging on, in desperation, to an ethereal being she had once painted in her mind. She was moving her body, in an attempt to snuggle between his limp arms, when she was bolted out of her reverie and found herself back in Tripoli, in the pediatrician's waiting room.

Her eyes sought out her husband and found that strange man cuddling his baby girl while, at the same time, calling her all sorts of nasty names.

She spotted him arguing with the doctor, "How could you name your own flesh and blood a cocotte and a harlot?" the female doctor asked.

"Oh! Come-on Doc! It's no big deal!" replied the bulky father.

Dr. Mona was not at all pleased with the response. "Well, a child is a gift from God and he or she, should be taken care of properly; physically, psychologically, and emotionally!"

But, the father insisted, "Oh Doc! She's the product of two thrusts, a tremor and a blank stare. She is not even worth taking care of!"

It was only now and then that the man's wife understood the meaning of those words. "Is that it?" She kept on repeating to herself, "Two thrusts, a tremor and a blank stare!"

It was only now that she understood what happened on that other night, in that hotel, in that particular room, with that same strange man.

13

THE WEDDING NIGHT

It was Tuesday, October 19th, 1957. Her concerned father stood outside her open bedroom door. With one glance, he assessed the room's contents as well as its single occupant.

Father and daughter's eyes locked together. He raised his eyebrows as a sign of apprehension; she smiled as an indication of bliss. His eyes assailed her with questions; her eyes responded with soothing answers. He knew she was intent on marrying the man waiting in the huge illuminated hall. She knew he opposed her decision. He was fully aware that she saw her posterity in that chubby male. She was entirely conscious of his disapproval. He understood her infatuation. She noticed his doubt; yet, she was drunk with joy, blinded with love. She blinked at her father in an attempt to reassure him and continued with her preparations. Her father turned away, tears filling his eyes. His shoulders sagged with grief for he foresaw his daughter's ill fate. He felt this weird feeling tug at his core, but, unfortunately, he had lost the battle.

She stood there, amidst the white flowers, dressed in her white lace wedding gown. She gazed at the camera, looking fixedly at the future which goggled at her through the artificial eye. By the time she finally noticed the hungry and cruel look the stranger gave her, she was already proclaimed his wife. For the first time since she met him, she carefully studied his face from forehead to chin, from ear to ear. She froze, suddenly not breathing. Strikingly odd questions assaulted her brain; "Am I going to face Ruba's fate? Am I going to be raped on my wedding night or am I going to be just another lonely Lina or another unsatisfied Miriam or another befooled Karen?"

She felt confused and terrified. She sought her father's eyes again and, in complete silence, their hearts fastened, their souls clutched, and her lips murmured, "I wish I had given into your assailing eyes."

14

THE SOURCE OF LIFE

The gigantic mansion stood in the middle of corn fields. Its overwhelming frame presided over immense and vast meadows. Even its shadow dominated its surroundings, devouring every flicker of light, obscuring all the neighboring pastures.

A mellifluous wind whispered in the ears of the servile peasants scattered amongst the vegetation. Men ploughed and cultivated. Men turned the land over. Men swept glittering droplets of sweat from their foreheads. And, men also listened to the soothing murmurs of the breeze that related stories of freedom and joy.

Meanwhile, women floated upon the wings of a soft gale, gliding on grass with jars of fresh water held in perfect balance upon their heads. Beneath their urns, their hips swung back and forth in harmony, teasing, inviting, and challenging the world's greatest beauties. Their tanned hands grasped the hems of their colorful dresses, uncovering shapely ankles. Silky shawls accentuated their slender waists, hugging their delicate figures with tenderness. Hips, hands, ankles, waists, figures, all seemed to conspire against the robust, sweaty men whose heads sprung upward whenever the sweet female smell tickled their nostrils. All men were thirsty. All of them craved fresh water but at the same time both men and women longed for the essence of life. They longed for freedom. They craved to quench their thirst but the indomitable structure that hovered over the fields obstructed their way to liberty.

The wind grew stronger. The whisper became a growl. The swaying altered. Arms, legs, and bodies shivered. Eyes were mesmerized, ears pinned, feet immobile. A piercing shriek ripped the air and the hearts of all who heard it— In the house's pool, floated the corpse of a ten-year-old boy. Death had struck unexpectedly and stabbed the predominating, lifeless edifice in its heart.

Days passed, which turned into months, and, still, the fountain of sustenance remained prohibited. Still the craving was not satisfied and still the wind blew, murmured, caressed, and whispered enchanting songs of freedom.

Then, one day, the wind carried to the fields the meek cries of a tiny, little creature. Choked sobs shook the plants. Feeble weeping made hearts tremble and hands quiver. The moans grew closer by the moment as they approached the vigorous, masculine arms, and the swinging hips. Time, nature, men, women, children, and animals all stood still. Suddenly, a white, tiny bundle appeared through the dense foliage. The package was tossed into sunburned arms. Unsteady fingers explored the bale. They unfolded layers and layers of white sheets, until two innocent, yet already tormented brown eyes became visible to curious and inquisitive gazes. The tanned, bronzed arms hugged the baby girl lovingly. Due to her gender, she was also forbidden to drink from the spring of life. The womb which carried her for nine months in a row, denied her existence. After all, she was nothing but an insolent female. How dare she replace him? He, the perfect ten-year-old male who was to be the heir, how dare she defy the callous construction's will?

Life in the meadows remained the same for five long years. The little girl grew among the ploughing arms and the playful hips, listening at the same time to the tunes and snarls of the immense manor which, from a distance, commanded and manipulated her existence.

On one stormy thunderous night, her sentence was pronounced. White, ivory arms stretched across the fields and stole her from the strong, hairy chests she nestled against. They snatched her from the warm, soft breasts from which she suckled for five years only to throw her into the embrace of cloistered arms.

For nine years, she was confined within the dark, greasy walls of an abbey. For nine years, she searched her dreams desperately for the mannish hands and the swaying figures but to no avail. Their memory faded away, only to be replaced by stiff, shapeless, and colorless ones. She lost track of time. Did she spend nine months or nine years in seclusion? She was not sure anymore. Time in that cold, murky structure did not exist for even time could not survive the solitude and the isolation which haunted the corridors of the convent.

She spent her days and nights trying to recollect the enchanting moments she shared with the peasants in the fields. She missed the caressing strokes of the wind. She longed for its soothing murmurs. She even yearned for the brays of the feared mansion. She wondered, at some point, whether the powerful arms that once held her securely ever existed. She doubted the presence of the delicate, harmonious shapes that nursed her for five years.

In the darkness of her hole, she sat alone and listened to the sound of silence. Once in a while, she listened to her heartbeats. She learned to enjoy the only music that was allowed her. She counted the beats. She danced to their rhythm. She sang to their tempo. She befriended ants and cockroaches. She allowed them to creep up her legs and arms just so she would not forget the sensation of being touched.

She forced her eyes to pierce the gloom which engulfed her room. At first, she saw only the cavities and cracks which covered the walls. Later, her vision escaped the panels of cement and traveled until it reached the green fields where she once knew happiness. Her eyes always explored and examined the dense vegetation all about in search of the once-loved humans.

She was just getting used to her situation when she heard a strange voice pronounce a new sentence. She overheard the voice say that since she was now fourteen, it was about time for her to get married. She was only fourteen and still the fine, supreme hands pulled her strings. They planned, organized and set her destiny. This time, they penetrated the lifeless walls, grasped her once more, and tossed her into the arms of a strange male creature.

Fortunately, fate was on her side. For the first time in her life, she was finally allowed to quench her thirst from the well of love. For the first time, her eyes sparkled with happiness, her lips smiled with delight and her heart danced with elation. She was in love. She found her source of life. She was free to laugh, talk, tease, feel and live. She had her own house, a cozy, warm, and comfortable place which she shared with her husband. Tapestries covered her walls, silk covered her bed, carpets were scattered upon her floors, and laughter filled her home.

The sensational aroma of her love permeated her neighborhood. She sprinkled smiles on her way to the grocer. She spread contentment on her way to the butcher. She shared chuckles on her way to the baker. She made heads turn, eyes shine, mouths grin, cheeks blush, and hearts quiver when she stood daily on her doorstep awaiting her beloved to come home. She even had the privilege to give life. She bore her lover's children, three of them. She became acquainted with the motherly emotions. She saw in her mate the father whom she had never met. She drank from the pit of love for twenty beautiful years.

However, the shadow of death hovered around the happy couple until it mercilessly desiccated her only source of life. Once more she had to experience pain but this time it was different. It was excruciatingly unbearable. Her dearly-loved was withering away day by day. She had to be strong, yet she was weak. She had to smile, yet her heart wept. She had to utter comforting words, yet she needed to shout. She had to look at death in its face, yet she wished she could close her eyes forever. She had to lie, yet she longed to say the truth. She was tired. She was drained.

Eventually, the laughter died. The colors faded. All was black. All was colorless. All was shapeless. She was back inside the convent but this time it was of her own making. This time, she not only lost all sense of time but also her five senses. She no longer desired to see, no longer wanted to hear. No longer did she crave to be touched. She ate only because she was forced to and, when she did, she only tasted death. She breathed, but she inhaled death. At night, she wrapped herself with the cold, white sheets in an attempt to find some warmth but sadly that was stolen from her as well. In the morning, she tried to peep at the sun, but dark clouds swallowed its brightness. She searched the faces of her children for his face, but all she could see was hers. She watched her offspring, observed their behavior, scrutinized their movements, and monitored their actions but, still, she could not reach him.

One day, she decided to venture into the neighborhood in an attempt to find him. She went to the grocer. She visited the baker. She passed by the butcher's but her lover was nowhere to be found. She stood on her doorstep, waiting for him to return home, but he did not. She knew, then and there, that her final resort was death.

Although death destroyed her only hope, she was certain that its clutches were more tender and caring than those of the refined and threatening hands that determined her providence. She spent her days and nights praying for death to pay her a visit.

She had forgotten that she had lost her senses for she tried to make use of them again but she could not. She tried to listen to the silence of the grave. She attempted to peer into the darkness of the tomb. She endeavored to ravage the intimacy of the sepulcher. All her efforts failed. Her eyes poured tears. Her mouth drooled. She nearly drowned in her misery.

At last, after two years of praying, the cold fingers of death responded to her pleas. They reached out, seized her, and flung her forever into the skeletal arms of her beloved.

Amina* was finally safe.

15

THE HELPER

An irritated Zeina meandered in aimless circles within her spacious bedchamber. She had to find a solution. She had put up with him for five years now and that was more than enough. As she paced back and forth, Zeina thought about her children and a gust of pride swept her off her feet. She found herself straightening her shoulders and holding her head higher. She had done her duty and accomplished her mission. She had given her husband two healthy boys. But, now, it was time to end that disturbing and quite revolting relationship.

With a puckered brow, Zeina approached the four-poster, or the "crime scene," as she called it. She extended her right arm to touch the patchwork quilt. For a moment, her hand caressed the bedspread with tenderness. But, then, in a fury, Zeina snatched the quilt and flung it onto the carpet that occupied the heart of the room. She stomped it with her bare feet until her breathing became heavy.

Zeina's black eyes inspected the bed linen. They then moved from the sheets up to the two, soft pillow headrests where they stopped and stared. In a fury, Zeina grabbed the pillows and hurled them across the chamber. The cushions hit the wall and collapsed on the bedroom's tiles. Zeina then attacked the sheets. She struggled to pull them off the bed, pulling them off in a frenzy. She started biting the sheets as if to tear them to pieces. She stopped, immobilized, when she found herself staring at the mattress. This thing witnessed her nightly torture. Unleashed, Zeina poured all her fury and resentment onto it, throwing herself on the pallet and pounding the feather-stuffed canvas with her fists. Finally, she gave way to her blazing tears.

Karima, Zeina's chambermaid, opened the door at a snail's pace, for she was well acquainted with her employer's mood swings, and quietly slipped into the room. Zeina, sensing her presence, looked around to gaze at her helper and then buried her face in her hands.

Zeina raised her head again to inspect the obedient woman standing in front of her. There was her solution! It was always there, so close to her, but she'd never considered it before. Karima was her way out of misery and despair. Karima was the maid and she, Zeina, her mistress. Therefore, she could do whatever she pleased with her. She assessed the young woman once again. Karima was of medium height and curvy around the hips but her features were exquisite. She was a gentle and sensitive woman who could even be comical at times. In addition, she was compliant, well-mannered and considerate. All in all, she would make a wonderful concubine!

Zeina winked at Karima and signaled her to come forward and sit next to her on the naked bed. Surprised, her personal helper advanced with caution and sat on the rug placed by Zeina's feet.

Zeina put her lips to Karima's left ear and whispered, "Would you like to be loved and cherished?" The servant was stunned. She looked at her boss with huge questioning eyes. "I don't quite understand what you mean Madam."

I said, "Would you like to be loved and taken care of?"

"But, who wouldn't like that?"

"Ok. Listen carefully. I think that, by now, you pretty well know how much I suffer whenever Mr. Talal approaches me."

"What do you mean Madam? No, I don't! Of course, I don't!"

"Well, let me put it this way. I am a refined being. This sexual relationship that all people brag about, run after, and get married for, doesn't mean anything to me. On the contrary, I believe that sex is an animalistic and repulsive act."

Karima knew exactly what was coming and she couldn't believe her ears. She had secretly dreamed of holding Mr. Talal in her arms, appeasing his frustration, comforting him, telling him that he was one of those rare men whom a woman would give up anything for just to stay by his side. Karima was in love and here was her rival handing to her the man she most desired, as if she were handing her a bottle of shampoo. "Here, you take it." At this particular moment, Talal stepped into the bedchamber to find Zeina and Karima shaking hands...as if closing a business deal.

16

THE PULSATING CARCASSES

A shadowy, obscure dirt track dug its way through the throbbing city of Tripoli leading pedestrians, bikers, and joggers to the foot of a mountain of jumble and debris. Anyone reaching the bottom of that musty hill was assailed by an unbearable, reeking stench. The odorous knoll forced all adventurers to retreat and turn their noses towards the more familiar stench of the polluted city. On the other side of this heap of debris, stood a twisted figure that always pricked up her ears to the echo of the treads of those passing by. The resonance of a long-forgotten civilization reverberated deep down into the hollow, empty heart of the woman as if the bells of death were declaring doomsday.

Umm Nabeel has stood in that same spot every day for the past thirty years. At first, her stance was erect and proud, over time, merely expectant and hopeful. Even now, she remains still, vigilantly lending an ear to every sound. When, finally, Umm Nabeel decided to communicate once again with her own kind it was too late, for nothing could escape her lips but silence.

Over the years, the old woman became faithful to her daily ritual. Umm Nabeel woke up every day at four in the morning. Her first impulse was always to reach out with a greasy hand to inspect the torn sheet for the battered and defeated body of Abu Nabeel who lay next to her. Once she was sure he was still breathing, she straightened herself up and stretched her numb limbs. She grasped a mirror she had found while rummaging through the mountain of garbage and stared at her reflection. Mirrored back to her was the face of an unrecognizable female with long, white tresses. Her face looked like a battlefield where deep trenches of wrinkles drew a map of horrors and atrocities on its old dry skin. A mocking slit joined her left ear to her right while two piercing eyes emitted signals of distress, the sole indication of the presence of the trapped spirit living within this aging container.

With a sigh, Umm Nabeel set down the glass fragment and attended to Abu Nabeel's basic needs as quickly as possible. She hurried about the shack, cleaned her husband's face with a greasy towel, fed him some crumbs of bread and offered him a sip of polluted water. She did not bother to change the ripped, wet cloth soaked with urine and rushed to her daily rendezvous.

She marched ahead with steady strides towards the lifeless massif while tears rolled down her cheeks and memories stumbled and collided in her crammed head. Her pace matched her thoughts until she finally reached her destination. Although the usual revolting odor engulfed the place, Umm Nabeel nestled against the repellent pile of waste and with a miserable voice related her story for the zillionth time to the huge pile of rubbish.

"Good morning, beautiful." Umm Nabeel opened her emerald green eyes to the soft and loving voice that penetrated her core and invigorated her body. Once again, she smiled back at her cherished husband, and held him against her heart in a warm embrace. "Hi daddy! Hi mommy!" Giggling and laughing, the toddler invaded his parents' intimate sanctuary to nuzzle within its rumpled sheets. The family threesome engaged in its morning routine of rolling, wrestling, jumping, and cuddling. Faces, hands, legs, feet, all became one. The four-poster rocked and danced to the music of joy and jubilation emanating from its layers. "Come-on, come-on, boys, stop it! It's Nabeel's first day of school and we don't want to be late!" Umm Nabeel swept her son into her arms and rushed to the bathroom. Abu Nabeel jumped out of bed and hurried to the kitchen. Mother and child were busy brushing, showering, and dressing while father fried his delicious eggs and squeezed a few soft oranges all the while whistling an Um Kalthum* tune. The happy hustle and bustle continued in every corner of the small house until everyone was ready to roll. They didn't want to be late.

It was 7 a.m. sharp and Nabeel's family was standing and waiting outside their community's public school gate located in one of Beb el Tebbeneh's narrow streets. It was exactly then that a horrendous roar pierced the ears of those present, obstructing their sight with heavy, black smoke. Shells streamed down like heavy rain, exploding, destroying, ravaging, and chopping. Desperate people ran in every direction seeking protection. Individuals disappeared inside shops and houses. Families were no longer families, their unity disappeared. Fathers hid under cars and mothers took cover behind walls while terrified children ran wild and crying in the midst of the horror.

A few moments, all it took was a few moments to turn lives upside down, to terminate a family's unity, to transform a living, breathing, human being into a pulsating carcass.

Then, it was over.

A deadly silence ruled the street. Wreckage blocked the road. Furniture, clothes, kitchen utensils, family pictures, blood, limbs, and organs covered the avenue. Buildings looked monstrous with dangling balconies, blasted windows, and disfigured facades. Slowly and quietly, human beings with shocked, expressionless faces started emerging from every corner of the street. It would take a while for the horror to occupy their eyes. Then, the realization of what had happened would hit them. The spirit of life touched their core once more, turning them into worried and caring human beings who hurried to examine the carnage and try to help.

All one could hear were shrieks and screams; all one could smell was blood; all one could taste was acrid dust; all one could see was scattered human flesh; all one could touch was cold and icy; all one could feel was death.

Amidst this devastation, stood Nabeel's family!

Abu Nabeel was there. He seemed ageless but his face was solemn. The light that once illuminated his eyes was extinct. The sweet words that once flowed from his lips had frozen. The hair that once was black had turned white. And the modest, spotless suit he wore was now a stained, bloody rag.

Umm Nabeel was there as well. The mother, who once hugged a lively child, now clasped that child's mutilated, lifeless body.

There was Nabeel!

17

CRIPPLED

The announcement read:

READER NEEDED FOR BLIND STUDENT
IF INTERESTED, PLEASE CALL 01/324489

Maya headed to the phone booth and dialed the number.

A warm masculine voice answered, "Hello."

The young girl hesitated for a second, and then replied, "I am calling to inquire about the ad."

"Oh!" said the voice, "so, you are interested in assisting a blind fool."

"Yes, sure, we're apparently attending the same university and I am willing to offer some help."

"Fine! I'll meet you tomorrow at 2 o'clock. I'll be waiting for you by the chapel's old Bunyan tree. You know where that is, don't you?"

"Yes, yes, isn't it next to the university's main gate?"

"You should know better. You're the one blessed with eyesight!"

Ameen sounded bitter and angry. Maya blurted a quick goodbye and immediately hung up the phone.

The next day, at 1 p.m., it was almost time to meet up with the student. Although Maya was well aware that the young man was blind, she carefully assessed herself in the mirror. The reflection she saw was of a beautiful woman with exquisite features. Black eyes surrounded by dark, thick, and well-curved lashes stared back at her. Her affectionate gaze slid down her face, evaluating two high cheekbones and a tiny nose which overlooked two full, pinkish lips. Then, her eyes followed the contour of her heart-shaped visage and rested on her long, graceful neck. They continued their journey and, on their way, caressed two perfect, delicate shoulders until they reached the deep valley that separated her twin breasts. At that moment, the eyes seemed to change color. They were still dark, but they looked gloomy now. They lingered, fearing to move lower. Something hindered their progress. Was it sadness? Was it pain? Or was it both?

After a struggle, the eyeballs overcame their terror to look at what lay below. "So, what!" thought Maya to herself, "All is not lost! After all, I've still got my eyesight. I still remember what they looked like. I can still imagine my slender and gorgeous legs, and sometimes, I even feel as if they were still there. Come on, come on, Maya. Stop whining. You have to move. The blind guy is waiting for you by the tree." Maya grabbed her crutches, abruptly opened the door, and left her room.

Ameen was already there, standing next to the huge tree, waiting for Maya to show up. Passers-by couldn't help but notice the young man. He seemed to be as stubborn and proud as the mature Bunyan which occupied the very center of the university, as it had for almost two hundred years.

Ameen loved this spot. Every day, he'd spend hours here… listening. Ameen listened and the tree listened. Ameen remembered the voices, and the humungous, wooden figure stored memories. Both human and tree, and in perfect synchronization, turned their heads to the left, enjoying the commotion of students coming in and out of the university. Then, a few minutes later, they mutually swayed to the right, overhearing the irritated words of enthusiastic undergraduates discussing politics. The debate, as usual, lasted for a while before the pupils rushed off to their classes.

Subsequently, the two accomplices eavesdropped on two lovers who sought refuge amongst the rustling leaves. And, they picked up the enlightening discussions of passing professors. Afterwards, the two partners indulged in eavesdropping into girls' talk. Finally, Ameen heard Professor Kareem greeting him and he knew that in five minutes exactly it would be two o'clock.

He wondered if the young girl was already there positioned in some corner watching him. Would she change her mind once she saw him? He knew he wasn't handsome but he had always been told that there was something attractive about the way he held himself. As for his deep, warm tonality, it never failed to attract females but, unfortunately, once they discovered he was blind, their interest changed to pity.

The wind whistled. The Bunyan's leaves danced to its rhythm and the tree extended its branches as if attempting to hug its companion. Ameen enjoyed the murmuring of the leaves and leaned against the old tree's trunk seeking comfort and support.

Maya spotted the young man. Goose bumps ran all over her body. Her heart sped up. Droplets of sweat formed on her forehead. Her hands shook terribly and, all of a sudden, she felt that she was losing her balance. She recovered with a deep breath. "Thank God, he's blind! Thank God, he couldn't see the cripple. Ouf! What a relief!"

"Hmm, nice perfume," thought Ameen to himself. He felt a warmth standing next to him. He turned toward it and said; "Hello, is that you?"

"Yes, that's me, Maya."

Her voice was sweet. Ameen relaxed and invited the young woman to join him on the bench, under the shade of the old Bunyan. They sat in silence for a few minutes and then Ameen introduced himself. He talked about his major; the courses he intended to take, and explained to Maya how she could assist him. Maya listened, enjoying the young man's inflection which warmed the cockles of her heart, and then agreed to help out whenever she was free.

Day after day passed, the aged tree listened intently to student and assistant. Its small buzzing world became a blur of Maya's engaging tone and Ameen's romantic intonation. The breeze carried the enchanting symphony on its wings, consequently blowing a contagious delight that reached every ear, touched every heart and spread a smile on every face. The ripened, living wood conspired against pupil and associate. Whenever the twosome nestled against its huge stem, it played its melody and Maya and Ameen reveled in its magic. For the first time, blind and cripple lent their ears to their souls, to the enchanting song of life, to the captivating tune of love. Their heads joined, their hands touched, and their hearts melted until they became one. She became his eyes. He became her legs.

A few months later, a group of students passed by the old tree, they stopped for a few minutes, watching what they called a "peculiar" sight.

A brunette sardonically asked, "What do they think they're doing? Do they think they can have a normal relationship like the rest of us?"

A teenager wearing an orange t-shirt added, "Most probably, they're just flirting for they can't be serious."

Another young man put in, "Oh, let them be! They have the right to fall in love. They're human after all!"

A tall and fair girl whispered, "They're simply disgusting. Look at them, a blind dude, and a...what do you call this, half a female?"

A muscular guy snorted, "Huh! You call that a female! It's some kind of creature, an alien maybe."

Everybody laughed and headed toward the university's cafeteria where gossip flared. The place buzzed with students. Some were having lunch. Others were trying to study. There were students taking naps. Many others were smoking. A group of students played at cards while others surfed the net, and many more moved about from one table to another conveying the latest idle talk to the eager ears in the room.

Then, to everyone's surprise, a girl rushed into the cafeteria and screamed, "Did you hear the hottest news? Ameen and Maya are getting married! Apparently, their parents agreed, but on one condition."

"What is it?" everyone screamed in unison.

"Maya's parents told her that if she really and desperately wanted that commitment, she will have to undergo an operation."

"What kind of operation? Stitch some legs to her torso?" someone mocked.

"Of course not! But she is to have a total hysterectomy."

"What is that?"

"Stupid! It's the removal of the womb and the ovaries."

"And why is that?"

"Apparently, her parents believe that a blind man and a woman without legs cannot afford to have kids."

Some students fell silent while others kept on talking nineteen to the dozen.

The next morning, Maya was driven to one of Beirut's hospitals. "So, what?" she thought to herself. "I've already lost two of my limbs. What difference does it make to lose a third organ? Plus, Ameen will make up for all my losses."

The hospice felt cold and insensible. Its white, bare walls sent shivers down the young woman's spine. The white, sheet-covered beds seemed frightening. Upon spotting them, Maya couldn't help but think of death, the death of her progeny. They were about to murder her unborn offspring and she was their accomplice. The nurse undressed her, in a rough manner, and helped her into a white robe. Was this her wedding gown or was it her kafan*? Maya stroked her flat tummy with a tender touch while she rested on the icy mattress.

Ameen was standing next to her, holding her hand and whispering some soothing words into her ear. But Maya didn't hear or see him. She had already retreated into a world of her own.

Would Ameen ever be able to reach her again?

18

CONDOLENCES

Aya walked into the huge and opulent living room to pay her condolences to the family of the deceased man. Her eyes searched all over but she couldn't spot the dead man's wife and daughters. So, she walked, with swift, long strides, toward an empty seat in the left corner of the room. She sat down, placed her handbag next to her on the floor, crossed her legs tightly and rested her hands in her lap. Aya then placed all her attention on her manicured toes.

Her cheeks were on fire; they burned with shyness. Whenever she had a social mission to accomplish – a funeral, a wedding, a baby's shower, or a simple visit – she felt disturbed, confused and lost. Aya always thought that this timidity on her part was due to her constant fear of violating some custom, what people call "social norms." On these occasions, her first impulse was to run for an available chair while avoiding all eye contact. She, then, studied her feet, with unusual interest, for the next ten minutes.

On this occasion, while staring at her toes, Aya was carefully listening to the conversations taking place around her in the various corners of the room.

Over on her right, she overheard a woman's squeaky voice say, "He, finally, divorced the bitch. Oh, believe me, she deserved it. She, actually, asked for it."

Another high-pitched voice interrupted, "Oh, come on, don't be so insensitive! "

"I am not!" squeaked the squeaky voice, "After all, he's of aristocratic lineage while she's...she's a middle-class slut!"

"Are you aware that he always fooled around?"

"Well, he is a man, and that's understandable."

"A 'man' you say. A man is supposed to be loyal!"

"What if she's not satisfying him? I guess he has the right to look elsewhere for someone to fulfill his needs."

A third woman joined in, "What if SHE wasn't satisfied? Doesn't she have the right to look elsewhere?"

The squeaky woman responded, "Oh, stop saying silly stuff! You know perfectly well that it's a woman's duty to keep her man by her side, no matter what!"

Aya felt green around the gills. The same reactions, the same comments over and over again whenever it had to do with divorce.

Aya's ears then picked up the conversation of two elderly women who were sitting next to her on a burgundy couch.

"Do you think he left a will?"

"I mean, my God, all this money! Definitely, he should've written a will."

Aya listened with closer attention.

"Hey! Keep your voice low. The old man's body is still in his bedroom."

"I am sure his wife is going to run the business. She's still young."

"What about his son?"

"His son is a retard. I heard he preferred his two daughters."

"You mean he left all his money and possessions to the women?!"

"Sure! Why do you think they took care of him during his illness? Is it because they loved him, or his cash?"

"Lucky women!"

"Hypocrites, in my opinion, they deserve to rot in hell."

"Ha! Ha! You're just jealous."

"Who? Me?! Nonsense!"

Shocked to hear such plain-speaking, Aya raised her eyes and, for the first time, assessed the vast living room as well as its occupants. All she saw were faces, faces without names. She preferred to concentrate on their words, rather than their features. For her, the identity of these human beings rested in their utterances.

The group of women sitting to her right was discussing antiques while three ladies on her left were talking about the latest fashion in town. Aya wasn't sure anymore if the man of the house was dead or still alive. All at once, she noticed that all the women present were not only wearing their jewelry but black designer suits and dresses. Their hair was freshly done. Most of them held a cigarette in one hand and a cup of Turkish coffee in the other. The atmosphere was quite relaxed.

Aya caught a glimpse of two teenagers who had settled down on a beige two-seater. An abstract painting hung on the wall behind them. Recognizing the two young girls, Aya decided to join them. They greeted her with big smiles and continued their chit-chat.

One of the girls was dressed in black and white. The other wore a plain, black dress. The latter murmured, "She's still going out with him, although she knows that her sister is in love with him."

The second girl answered with a mocking tone, "Sometimes, I don't understand women, or the concept of love."

"My dear, nowadays, it is not about love; it is all about money, cars, cell phones, and bragging."

"Unfortunately, almost everybody is falling for that."

"Look at Samar and Siham," spoke the first of the two daughters of the deceased, "These two are dating the richest and most eligible bachelors in town. Why do you think?"

"Because they're in love?"

"In love! I repeat, my dear…money!"

"But these two, in particular, are wealthy enough!"

"It's never enough!"

Aya felt embarrassed. She excused herself and moved back to her previous seat. She tried to concentrate on the grievance and pain she experienced when her father passed away. Tears filled her eyes and some strange feeling tugged at her heart. Did this happen during her father's funeral? Were people so insensible?

Engrossed in her own thoughts, Aya, at first, didn't notice the young woman standing by the door until the departed man's wife approached her. The young woman was holding several shopping bags. Apparently, she was a friend of the dead man's daughters.

Aya's lower jaw dropped and her eyes widened when she heard the lady of the house say, "Thank you Rasha! You're my savior. If it weren't for your generosity, I would've embarrassed myself by wearing my old black suit."

"Not at all, Aunt Hoda, you're most welcome. Here's that Armani you asked for."

"Did you, by any chance, find some shoes to match the suit?"

"Of course, I did."

"Thank you, thank you, my darling, now I can honor my sweet husband's memory."

Aya couldn't believe her ears. The woman's dead husband was still lying in their bed and the only thing the wife cared about was her attire.

That was it! Aya had had enough, heard enough, and saw enough. She rose from her seat and rushed to the balcony seeking fresh air. Tears filled her eyes when she noticed the bullet-hole decorated minaret of Beb el Tebbeneh's mosque. Chaotic and incoherent images dashed from every house, every street, and every corner of the impoverished neighborhood. Semi-naked children, battered women, drugged teenagers, armed men, demolished homes, and razed shops created a sad, despondent picture. Aya turned on her heals and left the nameless mourners to their small-minded pettiness.

19

THE PILLOW

It was the winter of 1978. Despite heavy Israeli shelling, many citizens were being evacuated from bombarded villages in the South on any vehicles that could be commandeered. A bus coming from South Lebanon parked in front of the Zareef* school, in Beirut. Once the Pullman came to a stop, people of all ages streamed out.

The men were few. They looked haggard and exhausted. Their bold, sweaty heads struggled to keep their kuffias* in place. Pools of blood filled their eye sockets and unkempt beards occupied their chins. Dust assaulted their clothing. Humiliation assailed their hearts. The battered men preceded the women and children off the bus, and automatically began by unloading the small number of handbags piled on the roof. Standing in file, the refugees then tossed the luggage from one pair of hands to the other. With every case and every toss, their heads, as if part of a single machine, rotated from one side to the other. Their shoulders touched, sending messages of comfort and consolation to their bonded hearts. Their feet grasped the ground as if attempting to find new roots. Their synchronized motion uttered the shame their thoughts couldn't consider and their mouths couldn't voice.

Silent children spilled out of the Pullman's exit door, terror painted on their innocent faces. Something had devastated their tiny universe. Grownups called it "The Enemy," but they, the kids, had named it "the winged biggie." When the flying monstrosity swarmed their sky, it swiftly altered their day into night, their dreams into nightmares and their childhood into adulthood. The youngsters assisted the men, each one of them grabbing a bag and dragging it inside the school. Boys and girls began standing at the threshold of every classroom, inspecting the area before settling in. Although the teaching space was appealing enough and practically equipped with all the necessities, it still seemed strange and alien. It simply wasn't home. Finally, the children marched in and occupied the mats that covered the floor.

Meanwhile, the women began stumbling out of the bus. They were jumpy and rattled and the epidemic of their edginess succeeded in reaching the men who hurried to help them with their shoulder bags, backpacks and purses. The women were weeping. They lamented. They grieved. They blamed fate for their misery. They cursed while hammering their chests with their fists, over and over again. They strode, in a clumsy way, toward their new shelter, mothers searching for their offspring, sisters looking for their siblings, aunts seeking their nieces and nephews, grandmothers asking about the whereabouts of their grandchildren.

While the other women sought and hunted, Huda and her newborn quietly withdrew to an isolated corner. Huda, a 22-year-old mother, hugged her one-month old baby with all her might and placed him on a double bed to sleep while she looked for some water to drink.

That's when she heard the unmistakable, piercing sound of an approaching Israeli Phantom supersonic jet. She ran back to the bed and lifted her one-month-old and hurried to the dining room where she hid under the wooden table. Agitated and sweating, Huda covered her little one with her own frail frame, embracing him with her feeble arms.

The heavy shelling drove Huda out of her mind and out of her hideout. She ran into the streets hoping to bump into her husband who had left the house earlier that morning. Holding her baby close to her heart, she threw herself down on the dusty ground and crept on her side until she reached the sidewalk. Huda pulled herself onto the walkway and kept on crawling until she arrived at the safety of a wall. The baby was still dozing, and his mother enfolded him with care and continued her advancement. She pressed her body against the wall and slowly moved along. She noticed a number of people hopping on a bus. Huda clinched her newborn to her and ran.

Huda jumped onto the Pullman. She shoved and pushed and found a seat where she dumped her weight and her baby's. The coach soon stirred. Amidst people praying, Huda softly rocked and sang to her infant.

The bus came to a stop and everyone embarked except for Huda who continued to squeeze and cuddle. When the motor vehicle was empty and quiet and all the citizens settled, Huda still remained, clasping and swaying.

After a time, Huda was ready to loosen her grip and breastfeed her son. She approached her baby with her nipple but he refused to take it. For the first time since Huda picked her child off the bed this morning, she lowered her head to check on her unusually calm baby.

She dropped her bundle to the floor. All color drained out of her face and tears flowed abundantly on her cheeks for many hours until, exhausted, she fell asleep.

The next day, some children found a young woman lying on the freezing floor. She was sucking her thumb and hugging a pillow.

20

KHADIJA, NOUR, AND FATIMA VS. THE HOURIS OF HEAVEN

Prologue: *Two months ago, I received a phone call from a seventeen-year-old who lives in Beb-el-Tebbeneh. She was desperate and shattered. Her brother wanted to force her into marrying a 'Salafi Sheikh' old enough to be her father. While pouring her heart out, she disclosed how young men in her neighborhood are brainwashed and recruited to join extremists.*

The adhan pierced the cautious silence that dominated the neighborhood. The Muezzin's tempting voice awoke Beb-El-Tebbeneh. People crept out of their beds (some of them willingly, others less so) and the daily ritual began.

Mohammad picked up his prayer rug and spread it on the floor's broken tiles. He straightened his back getting ready for the Morning Prayer. He mechanically raised his hands, placed his thumbs behind his ears, "Allah Akbar" ("God is Great") his lips muttered, and the "motion picture" began. Over the next two minutes , Mohammad bowed, straightened, knelt, stood up, bowed, straightened, knelt turned right, "Al Salamu Alaykom,"("Peace be upon you") he murmured under his breath. He turned left and repeated, "Al Salamu Alaykom."

His duty done, Mohammad reached for his machine gun and searched the house for his mother. He found her in her bare bedroom, crouching in a dark corner. Khadija looked up at her son then automatically lowered her eyes to the ground. The expected slap caused her nose to bleed. Mohammad's harsh voice which never failed to pierce her core, rasped out "Where is the money I lent you two weeks ago? You old bag of bones, you never pay your debts on time!" He seized her by her hair and dragged her to the opposite corner of the room where his sister snuggled against the cold wall. Nour awaited her savage blow with dread. It came with the words, "You're just another useless whore. You are going to marry this 'Salafi Sheikh' or else…. Do you hear me?"

Mohammad left the room and stormed into the kitchen where his emaciated wife was preparing their daily meager breakfast. He grabbed Fatima by her neck forced her down on her knees, barking, "How many times do I have to tell you that if I catch you eating before I do I'll just find myself another woman!" Mohammad threw his heavy bulk on a wooden chair, shoved a boiled egg in his mouth, and with one large piece of Lebanese bread he polished the 'labneh'* platter.

Once done, and once more feeling manly and powerful, Mohammad joined the rest of the gang who gathered everyday in the street beneath his balcony to glorify their hero.

"Ya ahla, ya ahla bi Abu Hmeyd; wlek ya heyk el rjel ya bala." ("Welcome, welcome Abu Hmeyd you are one heck of a man.")

"Ahla, ahla bilshabeb eltaybeh. Wlek taalamo elmara iza ma elkaf brakbetah shiber btflot." ("Welcome, welcome guys, you should understand that if you don't beat your women on daily basis, they will go astray.")

"Come on guys, forget about earthly women, and let us embark on our daily reverie. Let your imagination drift away from this materialistic world and imagine you are in Heaven. You are surrounded by your earthly obedient and submissive wife and her seventy, amazingly gorgeous 'Houris', and each 'Houri' is encircled by seventy other astonishingly stunning 'Houris'. And guess what? If you have four, earthly, dutiful and subservient wives, do you know how many 'Houris' you are entitled to? 19,600 'Houris' guys! And they are all dedicated to catering to your needs, to your pleasure. Do your poor minds grasp the concept? Can you imagine the scenery? Well, and there is more."

"For God's sake tell us more Mohammad! Stop the teasing, please!"

"Did you know that when you have sex with your earthly wife in Heaven the pleasure lasts for seventy years of our earthly time? And once you are done, you hear the sweetest voice calling upon you and seductively murmuring, "Ain't I entitled to some of that pleasure?" You look upwards only to find an indescribable beauty waiting for you with open arms. I can see that you are already there my friends. I think it is time to go back to Tebbeneh now. All this and a lot more are awaiting you if you fight in the name of God! God is most generous with his most obedient servants. Come on, let's get back to business now! Snap out of your reverie, boys!"

ACKNOWLEDGMENTS

The world is a better place thanks to people who share their stories. What makes it even better are storytellers.

To all the individuals I have had the opportunity to listen to their stories, or watch their transformation after sharing their life experiences, I want to say thank you for being the inspiration and foundation of *The Hidden Face of Scheherazade*.

Without the support of my family this book would not exist. Thank you to my daughter Rana, and my sons, Abdul Kader, Ramzi, and Rami for joining me on my ventures in the most destitute areas of Lebanon; thank you for serving others.

As for my brother Ziad Kebbi, thank you for being my rock!

Thank you to Gillian Piggott, my university professor, for believing in me. I will never forget the day you compared me to the one and only Charles Dickens.

Thank you to Mitch Ditkoff who introduced me to my editor, Val Vadeboncoeur. Thank you, Val, for your precious advice and added value to my "Scheherazade."

Thank you to Catharine Clarke, my book producer, for following up on every single detail. Thank you to Catharine and her team for unveiling *The Hidden Face of Scheherazade*.

About the Author

Sadika Kebbi is a corporate trainer and workshop designer with eight years experience providing customized training courses to the corporate world. Sadika is also known for her dynamic, inspirational, and unique storytelling style.

Sadika delivers career and growth workshops on such topics as Leadership, Coaching & Mentoring, Team Building, Design Thinking, Presentation Skills, Storytelling, Public Speaking, Emotional Intelligence, Business English, Entrepreneurship, Sales, Creative Writing, and English Skills.

As a corporate trainer, Sadika has designed, facilitated and delivered workshops for a wide variety of companies such as Averda (Sukleen, Sukomi, Leeds), Astrazeneca, and BLOM Bank.

Since 2017, she has served as a Freelance Trainer at World Business Fitness in Cairo, Egypt. In that capacity, she delivered workshops on Emotional Intelligence to associates of AstraZeneca at their offices in both Beirut, Lebanon and Erbil, Iraq.

After receiving the "Train the Trainer in Design Thinking" Certificate from the United Nations High Commissioner for Refugees (UNHCR) she worked, in 2017, in collaboration with the UNHCR and Nawaya, a Lebanese NGO, to train Lebanese, Syrian, and Palestinian underprivileged youth in Design Thinking.

Sadika holds both a BA in English Literature and a teaching diploma from the Lebanese University and an MA in Comparative Literature from the University of Balamand. Prior to corporate training, Sadika worked in the educational field as an instructor at Hariri Canadian University and Arts, Sciences & Technology University in Lebanon where she developed, implemented, and taught numerous courses. During this period, Sadika published an academic book, two research essays, several articles, and many short stories.

Sadika is also a John C. Maxwell licensed and certified Coach, Speaker, Trainer, and Teacher. In February 2018, she was selected as a finalist for the John C. Maxwell Stage Time Speakers Awards. In March 2018, she joined 250 other John C. Maxwell coaches, in addition to John Maxwell himself, in San Jose, Costa Rica to deliver a project called "Transformation Costa Rica." Sadika and the other coaches facilitated and conducted round table training for 15,000 Costa Ricans over three days. Sadika also conducted training for members of the Costa Rican Ministry of Finance HR Department, for Walmart branch managers from across Costa Rica, and for members of the HR department of the Juan Santamaria Airport. In addition, Sadika delivered a customized workshop for lawyers, doctors, and prominent figures within Costa Rica.

Sadika is a TEDx speaker. She was one of the TEDx Balamand University speakers on the 24th of March 2018. https://youtu.be/ee6JrASKiD0

Sadika is a member of the National Storytelling Network in the United States.

She is also a Toastmaster and, in 2015, was voted as one of the top ten speakers in the Arab World.

In 2017, Sadika launched an NGO called Kun Ensan (Being Human), which aims at building peace and bridging gaps between different political, social, and religious communities within Lebanon, principally through the vehicle of storytelling.

Sadika wants to use her teaching, speaking, and corporate training experience to fully understand the needs of people and help increase their performance and productivity in the world. More importantly, she wants to touch the human heart so that titles and labels fade away and eventually disappear altogether.

How To Order

The Hidden Face of Scheherazade is available through most all online retailers, including Amazon and Barnes & Noble.

Bookstores can order through the Ingram Content Group at www.ingramcontent.com

To order directly from Being Human Press, contact the author at www.sadikakebbi.com or email her at doukak@gmail.com.